Taking the Stairs

Books by John Stiles
The Insolent Boy (novel, 2001)
Scouts Are Cancelled (poetry, 2002)
Creamsicle Stick Shivs (poetry, 2006)

JOHN STILES
taking the stairs

NIGHTWOOD EDITIONS
Gibsons Landing, BC

Copyright © 2008 John Stiles

All rights reserved. No part of this publication may be reproduced, stored in a retrieval system or transmitted, in any form or by any means, without prior permission of the publisher or, in the case of photocopying or other reprographic copying, a licence from Access Copyright, www.accesscopyright.ca, 1-800-893-5777, info@accesscopyright.ca.

Nightwood Editions
Box 1779
Gibsons, BC, Canada V0N 1V0
www.nightwoodeditions.com

Designed by Anna Comfort
Printed in Canada

Nightwood Editions acknowledges financial support from the Government of Canada through the Book Publishing Industry Development Program (BPIDP) and the Canada Council for the Arts, and from the Province of British Columbia through the British Columbia Arts Council for its publishing activities.

Library and Archives Canada Cataloguing in Publication

Stiles, John, 1966-
    Taking the stairs / John Stiles.

ISBN 978-0-88971-221-8

    I. Title.

PS8587.T554T35 2008   C813'.6
C2008-900297-0

for Bob, Bonnie, J. Jonah and Boo

PART ONE

Daisy, Daisy, give me your answer do
I'm half crazy, all for the love of you
It won't be a stylish marriage
I can't afford a carriage
But you'll look sweet upon the seat
Of a bicycle built for two.
　—from "Daisy Bell," by Harry Dacre (1892)

✴ PANDORA'S BOX? ✴

"Are you alone, Jarod?" It was afternoon, hours before supper. I was half asleep.

I took the phone, cupped my hand over the receiver. I crept into the hallway, listened for Dar—had she picked up the downstairs phone, was she listening in? I could imagine my mother, under the basement stairs, head to the side, mid-rummage: *Jarod? Is that girl calling again? Not that one. Not Lana Banana!* But my mother wasn't frozen like a statue, ears pricked. She was beating cobwebs from the cellar ceiling. Thumping mud off George's boots.

"Not alone, but we can talk." I was tired, just out of my bedroom, savouring an afternoon alone with George still at school. I wasn't sure what to expect. I was never sure what to expect with Lana—I wasn't expecting her to call, anyway.

"Can I ask you something?"

"Sure." I sat down on the chair in my father's study, brushed the cat off. Minnie, a white barn cat, scowled then hopped over the dustbin and was gone.

"*Anything?*" Her pitch changed. I was certain that I could hear Lana gulp, as if she was taking in a drink of water.

"Mostly anything."

"I need to know something…"

"Okay."

"*Umm.*" Her voice hemmed and hawed. The silence was uncomfortable. It was the silence of restraint, the silence that occurs when there are many people in a room, not saying anything.

My mind started to wander. I started to panic. Why? I don't know. It was like I was waiting for something important to be said. What? I don't know. Was this the moment I'd been dreading? Was Lana about to dump me? Where was Rachel? Was my sister spying on me—in my moment of embarrassment?

I peeked out into the hallway, then returned to the study with the phone still cupped in my hand. No, that couldn't be. Rachel was at a friend's house, studying. I was alone, the sole occupant of the second floor, rattling around like a loose bottle on a school bus.

But I wasn't alone, was I?

Lana was quiet, just a hint of suppressed breath. I could picture her face, her hesitation. Why had she called? Did she have a secret she wanted to share? I imagined her hovering over an ornate music box, fingers poised, wondering, *Should I tell Jarod?* I looked at the receiver as if it were an alien being, as if it were an intruder, which had broken my perfect state of isolation and happiness. In the panic of the moment, I imagined all the horrors of the world about to be released from that box, into her little bedroom.

"Jarod? Are you afraid of losing anything?"

"Um, I'm afraid of losing my marbles… I mean, I'm afraid of going insane. But I don't think I'm going insane."

"Oh?" I'd lost Lana.

"You?" I was spooked, but relaxing marginally.

"I'm afraid of losing my mother. If I lose her what will I do? I'll be an orphan, Jarod."

How could she think such a thing? Lana's mother wasn't sickly, didn't drink or haunt the Legion. She was a nice lady, well liked. Lana's mother drove her to her singing lessons, patiently waited for her in the lounge, paid for them with a postdated cheque she earned from a home sales business. She doted on her daughter. It was impossible to conceive that they would *ever* be separated—yet, in a moment's panic it was possible that something, *anything*, could happen.

It wasn't fair, this conversation, this situation. I was just trying to relax in my room and I was being put in a position I couldn't improve on or solve. Still, I didn't wish to come across as a weakling.

"You won't be an orphan, you'll have me."

"Jarod!" Suddenly the voice rose like a call in the dark.

"What if I lose my singin' voice, what will I do?"

"You won't lose your voice, Lana."

"How can you be sure?"

"I'm certain of it, Lana. It won't happen, it can't happen."

"Do you promise?"

I tried to say the right thing to console her.

Um. Um. Um.

"Lana. You won't, okay?" Silence on the other end.

My eyes searched the ceiling. I didn't speak. Nothing came. Dar took the downstairs phone, put it down.

I wanted to say something, but nothing came. What more could I do?

✳ SUFFOCATION ✳

I was seventeen(ish), a quiet, slightly overlooked boy, who had caught the eye of the hometown princess. Was it a dangerous thing? In a way it was. I wasn't dangerous—I was quiet, looking for affirmation from my own mother, hanging off her coattails far too long into my adolescence. I was growing up fast, filled with nerves and my own hysterical imaginings. I knew, in the adolescent way, that a sarcastic remark to a substitute teacher could incite a fistfight in the hallways of the school, that there was a fire burning within me. Not a fire of hatred or mean-spiritedness but a fire of desire: to ask, to ponder, to know.

Our parents were strict; not mean but *careful, concerned*. My mother Dar was a school teacher (and Sunday-school teacher), a compiler of chores charts (with stars, and a point system!) for her kids. My father Edward was an academic; he was calm, understated and haunted the library at work and at home. He was in the shadow of my mother, who ruled the roost—all three floors! But we were a contained family: content, soft-spoken, polite. From the outside, people saw us mowing lawns, standing for family pictures. It must have looked a miracle: such a nice family, so well behaved and so on.

But I felt gypped. I felt like I had been taken to a Sunday-school picnic with George and my sister Rachel and while they had run free, to play and toss each other about, I had been left standing politely with old aunts and church ladies. I felt like a dog that had been sent to its kennel, for the sake of being a dog and not for any other reason. I wanted to bark.

But still, I was mute, embarrassingly non-responsive. I barely spoke. I looked up, saw, evaluated whether I should venture a remark, saw that it wasn't necessary—others would, could, *did*—speak, and so lowered my head again. It was my own secret frustration. Worse, I was lazy. Unlike Rachel, who scratched away private thoughts in a diary, I didn't even bother to do that. I was a tagger-on, a hand-me-down, one of those people who is just there.

"Head in the clouds, not in your studies," Dar used to say.

"Why can't you be more like your brother? Carefree?" my father asked.

But I didn't say anything. What would I say? Yes you're right, I should be more like my brother? If I was more like my brother, I wouldn't always be asking questions, being annoying?

But I didn't need to be like anyone else. I had Lana, after all?

Lana. *Lana Banana.*

Well didn't I?

✻ SINGING RECITALS ✻

I wasn't allowed to go to any of Lana's singing recitals. This included lessons after school at the local university practice rooms and those held at Lana's house. At first it didn't bother me; I was naive about the ways of artists, or artistic people. My parents weren't artistic people, though they loved art: museums, CBC Radio, PBS Television.

But I was Lana's boyfriend. Why shouldn't I be allowed to go and hear her sing? At first I didn't mind—I assumed there was a great deal of stress and anxiety in the lessons, chat between Lana and the teacher that didn't include me. So I kept this private, didn't let on to anybody that I cared that I wasn't allowed to sit in on her recitals.

But it was a small town. People talk. They pass each other in the street, meet in the supermarkets, at church, exchange information, gossip, tidbits. So, after some time, people started picking at things. *Not allowed to go to watch her practise? Doesn't she like you? But you're her boyfriend—you should be there to support her.* My mind. It started going in circles, creating plots and possibilities. I was her boyfriend and she was beautiful, the dream of many young guys in the school... *Why was I banned from her singing recitals? Was this a cruel lesson whispered late at night between our mothers to try to convince me to find a new girlfriend or get a life of my own?*

"It's not you, you silly goose," Lana would tease. "It's me."

It's me. The words of the eternal put-down. Oh how they made me burn inside. But I didn't say anything. What could I say? Lana was doing everything I always dreamed of doing, singing in public, being open to praise and ridicule. Lana was going places, I was certain of it. And I wanted to go there with her.

"Seventeen is a miserable age for boys I'm told," stated Lana, teasing me.

"Oh?"

I looked at her with eyes that said, *Will you love me forever?* She looked at me with eyes that said, *Well maybe, definitely. Today, I do.*

That wasn't bad, was it? Was that so bad?

Certain songs weren't to be sung. They weren't in her range, her mother Elise Bannerton said. And who was I to suggest otherwise, or to offer any suggestions or encouragement? *Okay,* I said, *fair enough.* Then Lana's mother told me Lana wouldn't perform on certain holidays, as it was bad for her: *Don't ask. It's not the way things are done in the music business.* Lana laughed it off, saying she was a diva, after all.

I watched her mother. Her mother was always there, in the shadows, watching, calculating, smiling, moving softly. Her mother was like a big aunty at a picture show, just brooding round her little prize. *Where was her mink shawl? Where were her diamonds?* (I started to think differently about her after I was banned from the lessons. She wasn't a bossy boots, true. But she was something else—what, I didn't know.)

"Protective," someone said.

"Controlling," another.

So, being banned from recitals, I had my imagination to play with, to keep me from going insane. I sat in the boredom of my bedroom, flipping through encyclopedias reading facts about strawberries, chewing gum, anything. What else could I do? I imagined that Lana's voice was like a great chunk of amethyst, found in a seam in the bedrock of Cape Blomidon. *A find.* I could picture the moment in my mind. All manner of people, hovered over, clamouring round. What a time for—*a find. Call the newspapers! Phone the radio station! Bring in the mayor! Lana was destined for the big time!* Well? Wasn't she?

Then after all this hysteria (mine) and *hoo hah* (hers)… real drama. I was in Lana's driveway with an ice cream—Moon Mist. There was a voice, singing through the window—musical scales. Lana's dark hair, white sash and beautiful, angelic face poked out: "Jarod, I can't come out today. I'm practising for a barn dance over in Glennville. It pays good, I need to get it right."

Get it right? Okay. Righto.

So… no word from Lana for three days and I endured my time at home being given extra chores by Dar.

"Plenty of fish in the ocean, Jarod." She mussed my hair.

I retired to my room, was swamped by the apprehension, the encyclopedias, books: *Guinness Book of World Records*, *Guideposts*. My brother George sat on his bed, shone a penlight in my eyes.

"Get a life, Jarod."

"I have a life, George. Get the penlight out of my eye!"

George's teasing voice: "Lana is pretty, Jarod."

"I know that she is pretty, George."

George sitting on the bed. A raft of announcements: Scouts badges to get. Hockey players traded. Then George snoring away, in the dark. *Not a care in the world.* George. My carefree brother. Snoring away like a buzz saw.

In the morning, George, pajamas down around his heels, hockey cards thrown around like Monopoly money, a laughing glint in the eye. Standing, bouncing on the bed—a new, gleeful nickname for me: PHD. Me half asleep: "PHD? Who was PHD?"

"Piled Higher and Deeper, dummy," he said.

Can you imagine? My brother, me, this phrase: in books, magazines, useless stuff. *Piled Higher and Deeper in books! Plenty of fish in the ocean.* These visions, these ideas… Then Dar standing in the doorway, a great sleepy bear. "Get up. Rise and shine!"

I escaped to the bathroom, my thoughts and my own world. It was a place in which I was right to do as I pleased and was safe within. I dreamed of agents and a girl with long black hair, a guitar playing live for the local radio station. It was going to happen for Lana, wasn't it? Eventually?

When I finally called I didn't pester her about the Glennville dance, just kept the conversation light. We talked about her mother, the dog, swimming lessons, anything she wanted to. The next day we shopped at Stedmans for a nice classy blouse. I paid, didn't have any problem paying. I was happy to contribute to Lana's success.

Lana just needed a stage, the right people around her, surely. Well didn't she?

Um.

The fundraiser at the Glennville barn dance...

"Oh, Jarod!" Lana cried into the phone.

Well? What? My Lana... My Lana Banana!

You can imagine the pressure, can't you?

Word got out that Lana had bad nerves. No one said why, or how it had happened, just that she had faltered on the night. You can imagine it, can't you? A beautiful face and a classy blouse, mouth opening like a cherry Froot Loop.

"Off key by a country mile," the organizer said. "Girl laid a big duck egg," said another, dropping his cigarette into a stubby. *Lana? Lana Banana?* I hushed at the thought.

But it was true. It wasn't just me, my imagination running wild. *Duck. Duck. Duck.* The kids from the slummy apartments chased after her, the little scruffs. They tormented her in the smoking section at school. They were tough, didn't relent. (It was merciless, cruel to see. Mercy me!)

Lana didn't want to talk about it, even though I pestered her. How could she fail at a barn dance, all those mountain folk standing round in overalls? I didn't understand it. All she had to do was stand there and open her mouth, stare at the walls.

Oh the horror. The phone rang off the hook and I was excited because this was so exciting. This was my chance to talk with Lana with no one listening in.

"Oh Jarod, what is happening?" Her voice was filled with

nerves, seeking relief.

I didn't know. What *was* happening?

"Nothing?"

"Jarod, please," said Elise, taking the phone. "Don't come over for a while, till this settles."

"Okay." I could feel Lana's disappointment.

"For a while. Just weekends." I listened, was there more? Yes.

"Ed, too!" I heard her say to Lana before hanging up.

The line was dead, nothing.

Huh? Wait now… Ed? Ed Bannerton?

I was stunned. I moped and loped into the hallway, hoped the phone would ring, then returned to the living room. Rachel glared at me.

"Stop hogging the phone, Jarod."

She hopped up the stairs. I could hear her dialling in the study.

Silence downstairs. I looked at my parents.

"You, you stringy good-for-nothing. You I can understand," my father said, mulling the court report in the newspaper. "If you don't find something to do with all that free time and wasted energy, next thing we'll be reading about you…" He shook the paper. "Right here in the court report between 'Break and Enter' and 'Arsonist!'"

Down went the paper. "But Ed Bannerton?" My father didn't understand it. "That poor fool is harmless."

"Ed's bad luck for Lana," said Dar, packing clothes into a laundry hamper. "He'll just show up and make her nervous."

"He's her father!" my father exclaimed.

✸ THE DREADED ED BANNERTON ✸

Ed Bannerton organized poetry and writing seminars at the Olde Cherry Tree Inn, in town. He had a bad name with the locals cause he owed money all over. Mainly on a grocery tab down at the Riteway and more to a fellow that sold furniture and second-hand televisions behind the Petro-Can station. Seeing Ed Bannerton creep around the back with all that muck and oil and gas didn't make it look any better. He looked like he came to pay debts on rainy days.

Ed Bannerton was a good-looking man at one time, but the years hadn't been good to him. Dar was more callous.

"Looks like an overworked school teacher," she said. "One that has stumbled out of the classroom and can't find his way back in."

I was riveted by Ed, the first time I saw him. He wasn't handsome, he wasn't tall, and he wasn't anything special. But he had a certain aura about him, as if he was good at being the way he was.

I couldn't describe it exactly but was he a fantastic example of failure? And if he was, was Ed the reason why Lana failed, because she saw herself as a failure too? I could only speculate. I was a teenager and not a very impressive one. I asked Dar about this.

She had that look in her eye. "You know what Christ did, don't you?"

"No."

"Christ always answered a question with a question."

True. I'd heard this before and I wasn't in the mood for Dar's games with the Bible or biblical teachings. It could be murder, with my mom.

"Was Ed an example of failure? Did he look like a failure to me? What was a failure in my eyes?"

Oh, the questions! My mother just gave me that look. It was her way of saying *I'll teach you for asking annoying questions*. My father, perhaps bored of the stalemate, butted in.

"He hasn't got what he thinks is his due in life," Dad said.

Dar added, "He hasn't got what he hasn't *earned*, Edward."

I didn't understand what Dar meant till my father peeled away an ever-present sheet of newsprint.

"Money," my father said through clenched teeth.

✷ THE TALENT SHOWCASE ✷

The Talent Showcase came every year. It was quite the do. Cars parked in the streets outside the university auditorium. Pylons lined driveways and side roads. RCMP officers pointed, flashed faces. People drove slow. People that didn't even read the newspaper crept up over the mountain in their rust-buckets, stole into the parking lot like shy animals. Cars lined the ridge road like fireflies in the night. They just kept coming.

Lana was like Snow White two years before and she won the competition. She was only fourteen. People talked about her grace, her poise, her moist lips. They talked about what she was wearing, chiffon. Her mother hovered over the proceedings. She was all dolled up. It was all flash bulbs and a night of glamour. *Where were the mink shawls, now? The diamonds?*

The next year, people sat mesmerized in the university auditorium as if they were parked on a ball field watching fireworks. I remember it well, it was the first time that Lana took an interest in me—I was there with Dar, who knew Lana's mother a little. Lana was this pretty little girl who seemed oblivious and I was too shy to talk to her.

"Are you singin' too?" she asked that night.

"No," I said, looking at Elise who was smiling at me. "Just here to listen."

"Hope I don't get nervous."

"You won't!" I said. How could I have known, that?

It was a lazy beautiful evening. The little dark-haired girl came out to the front of the stage and took her second straight award. There were no bad feelings, no jealousy or bitterness. Afterwards people drove from the auditorium, honking their car horns in appreciation and contentment. They had soft lazy smiles and sparkles in their eyes. It was like time stopped, a day of summer nights forever.

But that was last time. It was all different now. Lana wasn't the only little girl in the village was she? There were others, too. Surely they deserved a chance as well. After all it was a talent show, not a beauty pageant.

Competition brought out the best in people, didn't it?

The lady at the post office looked over her glasses. "Lana? Winning once was good. Twice admirable, but three times running?"

Oh Lana! Why now? Why this?

✳ SALLY ANNE SMITH ✳

The Town of Glennville Firemen—who had Lana ride on their float the year before—were now siding with someone else because Reg, the fire chief, played piano for his prettiest, youngest daughter Sally Anne Smith. She had a smile that lit up the room when she sat beside her father at the piano keys. They had a little banter, father and daughter. They had a certain charm. Their routine was different from the note-perfect, dark-haired raven standing alone on stage with a pianist off in the shadows. *A little humour never hurt, did it? Who wants to stare at a porcelain doll? Especially one that croaks like a frog!* It was crazy, how people saw things differently after that *hoo hah* in Glennville.

Rumours started almost overnight—in the crackling of the party lines, faces bent low at the Tupperware parties, lipstick smeared on mirrors. Maybe Sally Anne (little miss fancy pants!) had what it takes. *Who knew? Oh My!* Hands went over mouths. People leaned across tables, peered over shoulders, whispered. Sally Anne was *keen*, after all. *Patient… and ambitious. (Not to mention pretty.)*

Oh yes! People scurried into their homes, pulled the doors closed tight behind them.

Sally Anne had a little pep in her step now, everyone could see that.

"I have to give it a try," she said, a little coquettishly, sitting in her father's car. "Otherwise I won't ever know, will I?"

True. True. True. No one could argue that.

So what of this? How would Lana respond to the pressure? The signs were clear that she would fail now surely, weren't they? But what were the signs? Ed Bannerton? He was a spectre in her mind, wasn't he? A failure, stuck in her conscience like a great morose clown, grinning at her sadly, at every turn.

And me, her own boyfriend—what had I achieved in life? How could I help her? My mind it started going again. She must have felt so alone!

Elise Bannerton was all over the town like a cheap T-shirt. She was talking up Lana Banana in the bulk bin at Sobeys.

"You ain't her PR. You're her mother," someone spat. This, second-hand from George, hiding behind a hockey-card binder in his bed. Whooping under the sheets. Still, I listened.

Elise followed the woman out to her car, dumped her trolley. There was a squealing of tires. Elise tried to get the licence plate.

"Bitch," he heard her whisper.

I got a different version from Lana and Elise.

"All you need is family," said Elise passing me some watermelon. "The rest of the people are just businesspeople, or fans."

Okay. I agreed, but what about the locals? People who'd grown up with Lana. Were they just that? Fans?

They loved Lana. They knew her from the time she was a baby. They all loved Lana, didn't they?

Well?

So, drama and a big-ticket case of hometown rivalry. Who would win? Sally Anne Smith? Would Lana fail spectacularly, a second time?

Well?

On the night, despite her moaning and insistence that she was nervous and unprepared, Lana glided out onto the stage and took the microphone. She said polite and complimentary things to the town mayor and then she sang and won the third annual Talent Showcase anyway. There was a write-up in the local newspaper to record the event. Over that silly smile and that lovey-dovey look was this caption:

Lucky Ducky?
Can't This Girl Sing?
A Word to the Wise:
Inspired words from Carla Margeson,
your Valley Sentinel columnist

Isn't life full of funny stories? It is at this time of year that I reflect on the good things The Good Lord has provided for us and I reflect on the great way that our community comes together to support each other spiritually and artistically.

Just the other week, after I dropped off Carl at the Flower Shop, I was visiting a quilting group up in Brownville and I was sitting beside Miss Eliana Bannerton who was helping her grandmother, a quilting mainstay in the Valley these past twenty years, hang her latest offering.

It was a beautiful quilt, a patchwork gift to the community, celebrating the community ties with the transportation, pulp and agricultural industries, which provide jobs for our husbands and furnish our homes and enrich our lives.

Miss Bannerton caused quite a stir, seeing as she is now a Talent Showcase Champion three times running—and, it is rumoured—our next Festival Queen. A great many of the ladies were interested to hear Miss Bannerton say that she might be the first to be Queen "Lana Banana."

Now seeing as the name Lana has never fully been explained I asked this demure, modest young lady why she is called "Lana Banana."

"My mother says I once told Eldon Varney's eldest son I'd squish a banana into his face if he kept teasing me. So I did. In grade three. And he called me Lana Banana ever since."

Most of the older ladies were quite taken aback but then a ripple of chuckles went round. Isn't it funny how—even in times of conflict—humour can change our moods and affect our feelings?

I am thankful for the blessings and kindness that have been bestowed on the blessed and God-fearing community. I am thankful for the joys that are given to us in the talents of this beautiful, native-to-our-valley singer. I am thankful to report to you that Mrs. Jameson's quilt is going to be raffled off to raise money for the needy.

    Tickets are two dollars each. Three for five dollars.

Lana had risen to the top, won the Talent Contest and was proving that she could thrive under pressure.

    "Girl needs to get herself an agent," said the same voices that months, weeks, before had written her off. "Girl gets an agent then she'll hit the big time."

    "She'll have to leave the Valley," offered a few cronies from the apple boxes.

    "Leave the Valley? Shit, she'll have to leave the goddamned country."

    "There's always Toronto."

    "Anne Murray went up to Toronto."

    "Might as well be leaving the country, if she goes up to Toronto."

✷ FOOLING AROUND? ✷

I knew that Lana wouldn't stay, but there was a part of me that hoped that she would remain until at least she finished school. Ours wasn't a relationship that included anything other than heavy petting and fooling around and giggling between songs on the radio in the car, but it was something I cherished in the way that it grew from a single peck on the cheek to a comfort between us where we could open up about our feelings.

We sat in the living room. Lana was holding her mother's little pug dog in her lap, and looked at me. She teased the little dog, pulled his lip. The dog grunted and blinked lovingly at her.

We looked at the piano. Sitting quietly like a coffin.

"I'm supposed to be practising." She sighed.

"Do you want me to go, Lana?"

"No." Lana looked at me with that faraway gaze that she had for her performances.

"Do you think I'm good looking, Jarod?"

"I do, Lana."

Lana sighed, took my face in hers. She looked at me like she didn't want me to disappoint her, ever.

"I got my looks from my mum, Jarod. But I got my lazy, unfinished ways from Ed!"

Ed? Ed Bannerton, the enigma. I wanted to respond, say something comforting. But I didn't know what I might say, so I looked at her.

"It's not as bad as that, is it?" I asked finally. But Lana's face showed different. She just looked at me. What was going on in her mind? It was impossible to read.

✳ KISSING COUSINS ✳

I was into Lana's photo albums. She grabbed my hand, hopped up onto the couch.

"My grandfather used to sing." Lana looked at me proudly. "He was in a barbershop choir in Chase Station some years past, him and a bunch of men from the mill. He still lives up on the mountain. Sometimes Ed stops by to visit him. It's quite the drive. The roads aren't paved and there's no cable or nothing."

"I didn't know Ed was close with your grandfather."

"Sort of close." Lana was nonchalant.

"Seems a little sad, don't you think?"

Lana laughed a little. "Probably they talk about books. People used to say that Grampa and Dad got along better than Grampa and Mum. He's gone funny now, a little soft in the head. Do you know the song he used to sing to me?"

I didn't. Lana looked at me. There was no tension there, just a look that could go on forever. I could fall into that look. I think she must have known. She opened her mouth. She smiled at me. And then she sang:

Daisy, Daisy, give me your answer do
I'm half crazy, over the love of you

> *It won't be a stylish marriage*
> *I can't afford a carriage*
> *But you'll look sweet upon the seat*
> *Of a bicycle built for two!*

Afterwards, Lana looked at me with an embarrassed expression.
"A little corny, huh? The other one is a little sad. Want to hear it?"
I nodded.

> *Was a miner, forty-niner and his daughter,*
> *Clementine.*
> *Now she's lost and gone forever, dreadful sorry,*
> *Clementine.*

Lana looked at me. She laughed and she sang the lines again, a little crazier. "There's more, but that's the main part."
I nodded. I knew that. She must have known I knew that.
Lana seemed nervous now.
"Gram and Grampa Charlie were first cousins, Jarod. They met at a local barn dance." She laughed. "There's a little shame in our family. Every year at Christmas, family feathers fly."
"No one ever mentioned it to me."
"They wouldn't down these parts," Lana paused. "Buncha backstabbers."
She looked at me.
"Grampa Charlie used to stand at his window and wait for me to visit him. He looked like a big wooden soldier in

his overalls. He sat in his bedroom and stared out over the lawn waiting for me. His face was always smiling. He had a handkerchief he waved at me. Don't you think that is cute?"

It was cute. It was so touching. But I said nothing. What could I say? She said it all, hadn't she?

✶ WAYDE JAMESON ✶

I was in bed and having trouble sleeping. George was snoring like a buzz saw again and I hadn't spoken to Lana for nearly two days. Word was that she was in Halifax with Elise doing some important vocal work with a voice coach. When the phone rang, it took me by surprise. I darted for it, ignored my mother's chiding from the bath where she was getting ready for bed.

"Jarod." The voice was a young man's. "Jarod, it's Wayde. I passed my end-of-term exams. I just wanted to let you know."

Relieved, I sat in the chair. But still I was anxious. The call came as a surprise. I had tutored Wayde, who was a year younger than me, in English. In a way I felt proud of myself, though it was a secondary satisfaction seeing as it wasn't Lana on the phone.

"Good, Wayde," I said, hoping it might be enough.

"Yeah."

I yawned and thought the room was too cold. What would I say next?

"I have to ask you something."

"Okay."

"Can I take Lana to the Ox Pull?"

I looked at the phone in disbelief. I heard Dar splash in the bath, flip the page of a book. I heard her murmur. My heart, my mind, froze.

I tried to retain my composure, my idea of how to act calm.

"Why are you asking me this, Wayde?"

"Lana asked me. She wants me to chauffeur her in my new car. She wants to get dressed up nice. It's so she can surprise you and everyone else. I've been trying to summon the courage for a while."

This seemed a little weird, but still. Lana liked to keep things interesting.

"It's not my decision. Lana can do what she likes."

"Thing is she doesn't want to come in with Ed, because he might jinx her. And she wants to surprise you and everyone else."

"Okay." I had a hole in my stomach. Something didn't seem right.

"It'll be quite the do."

"Yeah," I said.

✴ BOTHERED? ✴

That part about Wayde bothered me but I didn't want to say anything to Lana. I lay in bed for a long time thinking about it, curling my toes and uncurling them.

It was a little embarrassing. I tried to reason with myself. Wayde was a nice fellow. I liked him, and he was even more immature than I was, so what could Lana see in him? I worried but I thought long and hard. It made sense if she was being kind to him—maybe they were related and he had missed telling me that part. I thought that made perfect sense and so I was also willing to believe it.

That didn't mean I didn't want her to tell me the first thing when I saw or heard from her. But the phone didn't ring and there was no mention of it in the school hallways.

I didn't say anything. I was attuned to her fickleness. It had a hold over me, so I watched myself carefully. I had to, didn't I?

✸ THE ARGUMENT ✸

When Lana told me she wanted me to come over after school my spirits raised. I thought: *This is it, she's going to explain everything! Wayde is just a cousin, isn't he? Or she's doing this as a favour to Ed, who owes Wayde's old man money. That could be it, right?* I didn't know. I loved Lana. I also had a great imagination. I was willing to believe anything.

"C'mon you silly goose." Lana took me by the arm and we left the living room. We got in the car and Elise drove us down to the river.

"No skinny-dipping," Elise joked at us, as she dropped us off by a fence near the house. We hopped over the fence and got down across a farmer's field towards the riverbank. The cows watched us absently. We sat down beside the muddy banks. Lana's voice was hushed, almost conspiratorial.

"Did I tell you I sent a demo tape to a cousin my mother knows in the music business up in Toronto?"

"No."

"Not too bad, huh?"

"I think it's a great thing, Lana."

"The man is some nice, Jarod. I talked to him last Se'rday. He says I have a voice and could do shows."

"The whole Valley thinks the same, Lana."

"Do you think I should go? I can't be down here forever. I'll end up like my cousin Myron. When he was young he looked like Elvis Presley. Now he stands on the 101 and waves at cars. I don't want to end up like that."

"You won't, Lana."

"Sometimes I get so worried, Jarod. I start thinking I won't be able to make it."

Lana had the look in her eye. It was a scared or proud look; I wasn't sure which it was. I felt a little inferior, like I was intruding in her moment. I looked down into the swirling currents, the little eddies like slipknots unravelling in the dark stream.

"You will, Lana. You have to make it."

Lana looked at me all serious. "What do you mean, *I have to?*"

"I mean," I felt uncomfortable, "if that's what you want."

She looked at me as if relieved and the tension eased out of her. I held Lana's hand. She tickled me on the forearm.

Lana took the reed out of my mouth. "One day you can write and I'll sing. We can be a real pair of cards."

"Just close your eyes and imagine that, Lana."

"Okay," she said. But when I opened my eyes, her eyes were wide open. They were staring off but not fixed on anything. They seemed almost dead, and the surprise of it shook me to the core. She looked right at me and she looked right through me. Was she holding something back? Was this the thing that she held deep in her psyche and wanted to let out so that I knew, finally, what it was that she saw in me, in our relationship?

"Never happen in a place like this. Not in this shit pile."
I was surprised by Lana's tone—so cold, so certain. I almost couldn't believe it. It was like she kept me outside herself.

"Nothing too special about this place, Jarod. Just people sittin' on their porches listening to the Broadcast News Report. People letting their trucks rust into their front lawns."

"That's bull."

"Oh Jarod," her voice rose. That hysteria, that look of panic and excitement. That same look of teasing delight I saw in George.

"It is not bull, it's true. This place is dying, the people in it are almost dead. Even the young people."

I looked at Lana. Something in me felt dead to hear this. It was the same as when I saw a friend from Scouts with a pack of smokes out in the smoking section.

"You know what, Lana?"

"What, you silly goose?"

"It's not over till the fat lady sings."

Lana looked at me. She laughed. Then she looked a little lost. "Maybe one day that fat lady will be me."

✳ PILLOW TALK ✳

George and I lay in bed and held our breaths under the covers. We listened for the sounds we might make, sounds of contentment now that we had finally decided to sleep. Dar and our father talked in the bedroom beside us, but their voices were muffled and low, like they were reading from the Bible or discussing a visiting neighbour who had dropped off a gift of bread or a bag of vegetables.

George and I looked at each other—we were like two shepherds under the covers, neither of us could sleep. George wanted to tease me and why not? That laughing glint in his eye... I was waiting for the penlight. Again, George? My brother, like a constant background noise.

I just lay there, a captive audience. PHD was now EWALN: Extra Weight Around Lana's Neck. The names were endless and I just listened to George, muttering, in and out. It was funny and in a way it was the greatest feeling in the world to listen to. I liked the banter with George, he was my brother.

My sister was smart, she dodged him. She was into her books, my sister. She avoided the teasing that way. "One day you'll be married and your wife will wrap you around her finger." Rachel, my sister. She had George's number.

"We'll see."

"You'll see." My sister was back behind a book. We were safe there. Our parents' voices were like the roar of an airplane: the isolation from the outside world, a cushioned inside world. But whom could they be talking about? We tried to listen to the words, to identify a topic, hoping for a raise in tone indicating a debate. Nothing. Just George. *Porpalorp.* Another word from him: *Porpalorp.* A Porpoise and a man combined. *Cripple cock.* A small penis that has had a seizure. George just smiled. He had the power, didn't he? To talk, to tease, to sleep.

When my sister Rachel made a sour face at breakfast, George and I knew something was up. "Mom and Dad have volunteered us to help out at the Ox Pull in September," she said, spreading marmalade over a piece of toast.

Then she added, whispering, "And last night Mom said she was worried you were going to get Lana Banana pregnant."

✶ THE OX PULL ✶

We didn't like the Ox Pull, us kids. It was too much work and it came every year, regularly, ritually and religiously. Dar took charge, became the Grand Pooh Bah of everything. We had no say in it, conscripted into the event like soldiers at wartime. It was her way of getting back at us for being such a family of whiners and complainers and do-nothings.

We liked making fun of Dar though, behind her back. She was everywhere, like a big broody hen, bossing everyone around. We joked between ourselves, us kids.

The Lions Club and the local churches sponsored the Ox Pull. Dar was in her element. Good was being done. My sister asked to be involved in a church skit almost immediately. Dar surprised me by saying yes. I couldn't believe it: was Dar going to let Rachel off so easy? My sister Rachel was so smart—holding props behind the scenes and talking to boys was better than dishwashing with a bunch of old ladies.

So that left George and me. I didn't want to work with George; that would be a nightmare. I had to share a room with him, share his thoughts on my reading habits as well.

But George had an escape route: the farm. They had a float that didn't take much work; it was the same giant cow and milking station year after year. Just a few tassels and frippery thrown on. Plus a few farmers' sons grinning like shit eaters. George was already an honourary member of the 4-H'ers. Rachel clever, elusive and away with her friends. George with his. Me, I got stuck with the bake tables.

"We waiting for the cows to come home?" Bill Crane, the barber, yawned as he pawed over a tray of date squares. I looked at him, grumbling away. He didn't have a hair on his head. If he had, he'd have cut it the shape of a bowl. He looked like a smartly dressed town crier, bald head shining in the sun. "How much for these, boy?"

"Buck twenty-five."

"That's highway robbery."

True. But still he paid.

Since Lana was expected to sing that night I was very excited. There was a great deal of anticipation in the air. People stood proudly on the tops of their cars, chatted in amiable ways with each other at the trestle tables, pored over the pies. Ox bells rang and clanged and volunteer firefighters stood proudly laughing with the locals, coordinating the fireworks to come later. Close to two thousand people from local towns and villages came to see the talent—the Eire Singers (a cover band from Boston), a barbershop choir and Lana Banana. Ed was coming in from Halifax.

I took the money from the bake sales and ferried between the tables. I chatted distantly with the old ladies while I looked for George who was with his friends down at the dunk tank mocking the local furniture salesman who was propped up on a seat. George slipped me a few sips of booze that the boys had brought with them and hid in the hay bales for later on.

I was in a daze of sorts, too much time spent in the sun and too much time waiting for my darling Lana Banana. The waiting was taking its toll and I was becoming irritable. Whilst the sweat settled and the swallows and nits and bugs dove in the sky I waited for Wayde and Lana and the motorcade of cars and village mayors done up in their full official regalia.

Suddenly there was a commotion down beside the stage exit where Elise had been waiting for Lana to arrive in Wayde's car.

Something was wrong. I could feel it. It was like when there was a lull in the weather pattern, when the peaceful air came to a lull and the quiet winds started to swirl round. I could feel the sinkingness in my legs.

This feeling turned to sadness and a slow burning anger when Ed Bannerton stepped out of his rusty old car and said there was no sign of Lana Banana at the house. Instead he'd met her grandfather on the porch in his slippers, waving a well-wishing card out in front of him like a handkerchief.

✳ FATHER'S CAR ✳

I took my father's car. I didn't think anything, I just drove. It was so silent in the car, my mind was racing. I could hear the engine hum like a cat purring in my lap, but I blocked it all out. It was a long drive, eerie, and everything seemed like it was lit up, like a storm had funnelled its way through the valley and I had driven into the centre of it without even knowing.

When I saw the little blue car down by the banks of the canal and the car door open, the socks and towels all flung down on the grass, I nearly didn't shut the car off when I pulled up beside them. I didn't listen for voices, I just ran down the pathway to the canal with raspberries and wild roses and blackberry bushes tearing at my skin.

Lana. I was whispering her name. But I was stuck on the other, the name of the other young man floating in the dark tannin river, pale white skin and blue eyes glazed over like a fish's.

Eulogy for Miss Lana Banana
Miss Annapolisa Drowns in Canal
Chase Station, N.S.

Firefighters pulled the bodies of two local teenagers from Murphy's Canal late Wednesday night, after an afternoon swimming accident. Wayde Boyd Jameson, 16, of Brownville and Eliana Bannerton, 17, of Chase Station recently crowned Queen Annapolisa in the Apple Blossom Parade were reportedly taking some time to cool off before Miss Bannerton was expected to appear in the Glennville Ox Pull, Saturday night. The tragic news comes on the tail of news of a harsh July frost and an infestation of spruce bud worm. New Babylonia Mounties report no evidence of foul play. Members of the Glennville Anglican Church Choir were heard singing late into the night on the grounds of Mercy's farm:

Was a miner forty-niner and his daughter Clementine.

Now she's lost and gone forever, dreadful sorry Clementine.

PART TWO

These were city people. They looked as if they didn't know they were in a fine car, as if they didn't know they were dressed up. Their eyes were like a dog's eyes in heat. They took little bites out of whatever they looked at, lazily, without even tasting.
—Ernest Buckler, *The Mountain and the Valley*

ONE

So back in Toronto, the phone is ringing, but I don't pick it up. A cynic would say that a depressed person would not have any interest in answering the phone but a depressed person would say that the phone is a distraction that takes away from the focus, the never-ending focus of being a writer. Generally this means keeping up on the hockey scores in all four newspapers, fantasizing about making a mint on the stock market, becoming an eyesore in the library and developing habits most people think are a little odd. People think it's odd if you walk into the corner store with your fly down, which I suppose is natural because my theory is that people are generally uncomfortable with themselves and want to believe that it is all good and fun for some people, the lucky people who aren't concerned about all the problems and inconsistencies of this so-called life. Those lucky people are the people who are happy to wait and take elevators. These are not people who take the stairs.

TWO

Phone rings and this time I answer it.
"Jarod, what's up?"
"Maury?"
"How's it goin'?"
"It's goin', Maury."
"How's life?"

I'm juggling two, three, things as I talk to Maury. One is an article I'm researching for a film director who is on hold. Another is a glass with chocolate milk powder all gummed up and stuck to the sides. I put the drink back on the desk but it spills onto a bio that I've just printed out to send to a literary journal. *Shit!* The other thing I'm doing is brushing the hair of Ade, who is, this moment, in my bed.

"Maury, I gotta go."
"I jus wanna cha… chat." His voice sounds so depressed.
"One sec."

The dark-haired one takes the phone. Double clicks.
"Hello, sir. Can he call you in one hawr?" Pause. Smile. Delight. "Oh, ees Maury. How are you Maury?"
"Gimme the phone."
Extra sweet. "*Bye, Maury.*"

I get tense. Click the phone again. It's the commercial film director from North Carolina who has been contracted to shoot for the animation house in Toronto that I do contract work for. "Mr. Jacob?" I trade ears. "Sorry for the wait. Six-thirty tomorrow morning is fine." Click.

A stare. Hellish stare. Tangled hair and blood-red lips.

"Yarud. You mean thees man is going to call you at six-thirty in the morning?"
"Yes."
"Why?"
"I didn't ask."
"You have to ask, Yarud. You could tell heem that it is awnly six o'clock in the morning and you will be fast asleeping like most people."
"That's why I don't generally answer the phone."
"What if is Momee, Yarud?"
"That's the exact reason why I don't answer the phone."
Adrieneese puts her hands up near her ears. Her fingers go in rings around her ears.
"Yarud you crazy you know. *Poco loco.*"
Crazy. Yes, I know. Crazy for girls.

At night I dream of Adrieneese sneakily poring over my manuscript about Lana Banana. In the dream, Adrieneese is telling me in various squeaks and pleased grunts that she thinks it is all right and I should publish it. I want to tell her that publishing it is not going to be easy. I have about a million things to finish and one of them is to try to keep her from leaving me, which I am convinced she will do regardless of what she might say.

Then there is the matter of keeping a job and there is the matter of Elliott, who is the biggest threat to the Lana Banana novel as he is simply an opportunist alcoholic/dickhead/weasel/film dude trying to cash in on my dubious ability to write for the screen. And he is not even producing in the film business; he is a soundman, a hired hand, working in a crappy video shoot, last I heard.

Adrieneese, in the dream, yawns when I say this. I want to say that I feel as if Elliott has attacked me with a poison dart. I am stuck in a web, a spider's web of dire finances, suppressed feelings and stifled creativity. Elliott is a nightmare of a human being, masquerading as an elegant and concerned friend. I am certain that if I leave Toronto today, I will never come back again.

THREE

Phone rings again. I'm on a roll and I answer it.
"Jarod P."
"Elliott?"
"I am driving straightaway to your house to present you with a book."
"What book?"
"A first novel by an author who killed himself."
"I'm just out the door, Elliott."
"I will leave the book on your porch?"
A moan from the bed. One eye open. "Yarud?"
"You have company, Jarod P.?"
"My mom is visiting. She's worried about me."
"Great. I will treat you to a late brunch at the Shoe Factory. I can't eat as I've just had gum surgery and I can't walk because I've also just had a vasectomy but I've yet to be banned from the place and I'd like to spoil you. How is your mother?"
"She's about to leave for the airport."

"Have the bags ready on the porch. I'll chauffeur you both."

"She's taking a cab, Elliott. Cab fare is part of the hotel package."

"Hotel? Next time have her board at the house with me."

"One sec, Elliott." Click. Dark hair on a white pillow. Stirring in the futon. Moans. "Yarud?"

"Yes, Adrieneese?"

"Who ees?"

"The film guy."

"What he want?"

"A piece of the action."

"Tell him you are spending the morning with me."

"I can't. I told him my mom is here."

"Jeez. Yarud, why you always gotta lie, eh? Tell him you weeth me."

I take the phone.

"Elliott, I've lied to you! My mother is not here. She is probably, this moment commiserating with some dying wretch in a nursing home down home. The truth of the matter is that I am with my girlfriend and we are just about to get up and make coffee."

"Hungover sex is the best."

"Bye, Elliott."

Down goes the phone. Adrieneese's eyes are open and staring at me, but she is asleep. This is a neat trick I note—trying to suppress the panic I feel at being behind in everything yet again—a neat trick that makes me feel slightly uncomfortable. Still, I love her. Any man would love this woman, whom I have now been with for almost a year. I am thinking this as I am staring at a business card on the counter of the table. It teeters there like a thrown playing card, scribbled on with snippets of dialogue, phone numbers, insults, a chorus of jeers. The card reads:

ETCH PICTURES
ELLIOTT BALE
PRODUCER
(416) 327-2243
(416) EAR-ACHE

I look at Adrieneese. She looks like a warm chocolate croissant, or a hot dog. I forget the building anxiety for a moment. A hand appears. The hand clutches mine. It squeezes. Warmth. A murmuring begins and I look into the source of the murmuring: a mouth that begs kissing. Still, I do not kiss. I am looking at that godforsaken card: Elliott Bale: Letch. Wretch. Money Pig. Ah yes, those last scribblings are mine.

FOUR

Phone rings again.
"Hello?"
"Jarod?"
"Dad?"
"How's my son?"
"I'm in between jobs, Dad."
"Are you broke again?"

"No, god. No."

"Jarod, the last time you told me you didn't need money you called me a day later in a panic and asked for five hundred. Are you sure?"

"Jarod?" Now it is my mother.

"Yes, Dar."

"Have you been out today?"

"I'm out every day. Walking the back alleyways. Hiding from people."

"Why have you been walking down back alleyways, Jarod?"

"It is the only place I feel calm. This city is like a big silent camera waiting to snap you at your worst moment."

"Have you been to church?"

"Not since Christmas."

"How is your love life, dear?"

"I'm still with Adrieneese."

"She sounds nice, dear. Will you marry?"

"She's an artist, Dar. Artists don't marry. They say the wrong things to one another and implode."

"Your brother and his wife are expecting. Do you know anything about being a godparent?"

"Only that it depresses me, Dar."

"They're very happy. Your godparents were very good to you Jarod. By the way, we're off to England next week."

"Again?"

"Yes, you know how your father gets."

"I wish I could come."

"So does your father. But you're too old for that. Bye, dear.".

"Bye, Dar."

The sound of the kitchen door shutting. High-pitched operatic singing. Someone teasing the cats. A gasp. A sneeze.

"God love us. Sometimes your mother infuriates me." My dad grumbles at me. "Are you sure you're alright for cash, Jarod?"

"I am."

FIVE

I am at a diner with Adrieneese and we are trying to be civilized as we tuck into a large plate of french fries. I notice that Adrieneese doesn't like to talk much and that her face is a little puffy and that she hasn't touched her coffee and that she has an intense look on her face when I ask her a question. I know that I do ask a ton of questions and this might have something to do with the everlasting expression of frustration on this woman's face. Anyway the good part about being with Adrieneese is that she has the same passion for sex as she does for food. The bad part is that she is on the rag again and though it doesn't really bother her I don't really want to hear about it. The other bad thing is that I realize I don't actually have any money when the bill comes.

"Do you have money, Adrieneese?"

A wipe of ketchup. Adrieneese lips. "Money?"

"Yeah."

"Yarud, why you no have money?"

Later we're at a phone booth near my house, near the old persons' home, up from the loony bin on Queen.
"Yarud, what are you doing?"
"Calling my father. Collect."

SIX

Adrieneese decides to spend the night at home and so I am free, finally, to get to work on this press release I am writing for the animation company. The place I work is quite the to-do. It is in a busy part of town, the fashion district. They have Renaissance prints on the walls, dour-looking men in jaunty hats; there are pretty secretaries in pigtails who smile at you in a concerned way, give you glasses of juice to drink when you come in and sit down with little interest in moving. I like going there; it is a place where you can forget everything, the predicament, the poverty. So I begin to get all the papers that are all over my desk and under my bed organized for the press interview I have with Leonard Jacob, commercial film director, at 6:30 A.M. When the phone rings, I wish I had five more dollars a month so that I could have call display.
"What up J?"
"Maury?"
"How's it goin'?"
"It's goin'…"
I listen aimlessly as Maury tells me about an author he likes and his own novel, which he is waiting for literary agents

to approach him about. I file and clod about the room with the phone in my ear trying to push the dust bunnies, rejection slips, Adrieneese's stale cheezies, socks and tissues into a corner in the room.

When I finally do hang up the phone I pick it up, again. I have a message from Dar. A musician I know from university is being interviewed on CBC in Halifax. Instead of feeling good for this person, I am miserable that it isn't me. In the midst of throwing a must-clean-everything-now temper tantrum I pull the towel around me, hang up the phone and stumble onto a short story I have never published and probably never will. I sink down in the spot, start flipping the pages.

I need to remove myself from all of this and live in a permanent imaginary world. It would be a lot easier. My idea of paradise: No-dick and I can simply exist as a hunched-over stork with a beer gut in a dingy room with the windows permanently drawn.

✳ COPIES: AN ESSAY IN CONTROL AND THE AVOIDANCE THEREOF (FOR ELLIOTT) BY JAROD PALMER ✳

Suzanne was bent on reforming me. And even though she was nice about things, we were pretty much doomed from the start. The relationship started with books, and I'm a reader so it was okay, that part, the book part, cause that's where we met, a bookstore, but Suzanne never mentioned anything about singing in public, and that pretty much changed everything.

Suzanne knew I read so she started buying me books. Week after week she came home with a white bag filled with the latest, trendiest bestsellers that she purchased at the Lichtman's at the corner of Yonge and Richmond. At the beginning, I graciously accepted these gifts from Suzanne—the magazines, the books, the little chocolate Hershey's kisses—and I took them home without complaining because, I told myself, I needed to change a few things about my lifestyle. It soon dawned on me that there was no way I could keep up with all these books piling up on the dresser table in my room, collecting dust. So I started giving these books away. One, *Reflexions of a Zookeeper*—a terrible book I might add—I gave to a lady down the hall whose legs are swollen.

I think Suzanne must have known that I was giving away her books, because soon after she shifted her campaign at reform to clothing which she bought second-hand off the racks at Exile at Kensington Market. Her preference for attiring me seemed to lie in loud, garish orange and blue polyester shirts, and the ones she bought me always fit me a little too tightly. But to be fair I didn't mind the clothes too much. Clothes I view as a sort of camouflage. And camouflage I view as an essential thing.

To be honest I was surprised that Suzanne was even attracted to me. I'm no looker, that's for sure. I've got a pigeon chest, and skinny legs, and a birthmark on my ear that looks, they say, like a map of Nova Scotia. But people say I'm pretty fast with the lip, actually pretty charming, though I've never in my twenty-five years had what you'd call a girlfriend.

The reason I know that Suzanne was charmed by me was because she used to hold her tummy when I was with her. If you don't get this, I'll explain it in relation to plays. I don't like plays. Never did. I don't like people who project their voices. I don't like curtain calls, and bouquets, and I especially don't like the idea of community theatre.

And one day I told Suzanne my thoughts on community theatre, because she was thinking of driving me to Kitchener to see a play that her friend Marion was in. I said who wants to see a play in Kitchener directed by a small-town snob who most likely immigrated here from England because he was a non-entity back home.

"Jarod," she said real quickly. *And she held her tummy.* She was shining inside, charmed. That's what I mean when I say she was holding her tummy.

The other thing about Suzanne was that she was obsessed with this singer called Alanis Morissette. She wouldn't admit it of course, but it was imprinted in the fabric of her daily routine. It was there in how she wore her hair (curly), what kind of clothing she preferred (flowing white shirts), and she had an aura punctuated by her mouth—a red rosy pout that would be a nuisance if she didn't know how to use it to her advantage.

Suzanne expressed herself in a series of head movements: head thrown back quickly, her hand gathering and twisting the skein of hair that flowed down her back, head tilted, hair pulled behind her ear, that sort of thing. And she loved to drive her car. Those are the things I most remember about her. Her hair and her car. The car was a red Tercel with a plush interior and glove compartment full of cassettes:

Meshell Ndegeocello. Stewart Copeland. And yeah, Alanis Morissette.

Suzanne got to thinking that her talent lay in singing—opera of all things—and was spending fifty, sixty bucks an hour on her voice. Some perfectly pleasant middle-aged lady in the Beaches, with an office like a dentist, with magazines put out by the Canadian Opera Company, was taking her money. Suzanne used to pick me up on Tuesdays at my apartment on Shaw Street so we could drive to the lesson together.

She put on the tape, her tape, the only tape that—to her—existed. She was patting at the steering wheel.

"Isn't it ironic, don't you think?" she said turning towards me.

"I hate that song," I said, picking at my teeth. I was sitting in the back seat.

"They play it too much," agreed Suzanne as she kept patting the wheel.

I put my glasses on. She looked at me through the rearview mirror, brown eyes blinking.

"Jarod, you should wear those glasses more often," she said. "You look like Harrison Ford in them." She screwed up her face. "A prickish sorta Harrison Ford."

"Jean Rhys." I said jostling in the back seat, waving to the street people. "I want to finish reading everything by Jean Rhys."

"Have to search the used bookstores," she said. "But anything for you," she addressed me as if I were a small boy, *"Harrison."*

She sipped again from the Tim Hortons mug. Gargled.

"Everybody thought Jean Rhys was dead," I said, thumbing through a book, one I'd bought myself.

"That right?" Another sip. Brown eyes in the rearview again. "But she wasn't dead—was she?"

"No." I said. "She wasn't dead."

Suddenly Suzanne stopped the car. She turned and smiled at me. "Jarod," she said, "I've got a surprise for you."

We walked into a tattoo shop. The tattoo shop was called Smiling Buddha, something like that.

"My treat," she said. "I'm getting us tattoos."

"Nope," I said staring with disdain at a cigarette ember with smoke curling to the ceiling. "Thanks anyway though."

"Jean Rhys. You could get a tattoo of Jean Rhys, Jarod." Suzanne was scrutinizing the walls. Bumblebees, tribal designs, a fat cat named Marvin, teardrops.

"You're going to be late for your singing lesson," I said annoyed.

Still she persisted. "It's the location more than the actual design, don't you think? What I mean is you have to get it in the right place."

"Tattoo your earlobe," I said.

"Like a Maori," she answered.

Boy I was getting mad. There was no getting to her.

"How come you never argue with me?" I asked.

"Cause I agree with most things you say, Jarod." Suzanne's voice was distracted.

"Let's go," I said. "I think we should go."

At the singing lesson I waited for her in the back seat of the car. Suzanne came back, mussed my hair. "Monique has moved

me on to *La Traviatta*. Want to get something to eat?"
I put down the book. "Sure," I said.

We were eating caesar salad but I didn't like the fake bacon bits.

"Who would have thought it figured…"
"Don't do that," I said, flicking little red bits off the plate.
"It doesn't fit."
"Sing?"
"Yeah."
"I thought you liked my voice."
"When you talk—sometimes."
"Prick." She smiled.
I was mad. Nothing was pissing her off.
"Are you Alanis Morissette?" I asked. I had a weird look on my face. I knew it because I'd seen the look in the mirror once when I'd felt this way before and I hadn't recognized myself. Actually I scared myself. I was somebody I didn't know—a weirdo, similar in appearance, vaguely recognizable but with a different look. Dark.

"What?" Suzanne's fork was twisting into an open mouth.

"Are you Alanis Morissette?"
"No."
"Then sing like *you*," I said brushing the anchovy bits off the plate and onto the tablecloth, and squishing them with my fork into the tablecloth.

"Sing like *Su—zhan*," she was waving her hands around her head theatrically.

"Whoever she is," I replied.

"You're such a prick," she said, *holding her tummy*. I picked my teeth again, squinted. Fuck I was getting mad.

"Your hair always been curly?" I asked.

"Since I permed it."

"Alanis's hair is curly, eh?" I had my eyes wide open and I had a humming in my head.

"Yeah," she replied real lazy. She poured herself a glass of Evian.

"Part of the mechanism," I said. I was staring at a leaf of lettuce floating in my Coke.

"What?" Suzanne sort of laughed.

"High school. All the popular people. They all conform to be part of the mechanism."

"Jarod, hon, what are you talking about?" Suzanne's elbows were on the table.

"Leonard Cohen," I said. "'Bird on a Wire' is the same song."

"As what?"

"'Isn't it Ironic,' 'Bird on a Wire,'—they're all part of the same song. Same idea. Just copies."

I spat the lettuce out of my mouth, and noticed that the white sauce had the consistency of cottage cheese. That brooding look I have was there, hanging over me like a dark cloud. "Like you," I said.

Suzanne's face went white.

"Waiter," she said, "can we have the cheque?"

We were in the car. "Jarod, you have to understand. Most people can't comprehend personality disorders, and—don't get me wrong—I more than understand personality disorders. But you just can't act like that in public, spitting out salad onto the tablecloth, and talking with your mouth full, and squashing things onto your plate."

"It's all coming to a head," I said, snapping my jaw tight, rocking my head back and forth.

"Jarod," Suzanne was shaking her head, "You know, when I first saw you in the bookstore I was sort of intrigued by you, by your intelligent mind and your absolute lack of awareness with what is going on in this world we live in, the twentieth century. But now I'm starting to see that you're just kind of a scared, bitter anachronism who finds fault with absolutely everything."

"I'm getting it," I was lurching in my seat. "I'm getting it, Suzanne."

"Like ra-a-iin. When you're already wet." I think there was a break in Suzanne's voice. But I was probably wrong; Suzanne was after all very theatrical.

"Copies," I said. "It's all about copies: tattoos, rock songs, caesar salads. There aren't any originals. They're just copies." I was batting my hands together like a crazy kid. I made a silly, mad, funny face. "Like you."

"Stop that, Jarod." Suzanne was grabbing at my hands.

"No," I said. "No way."

"Then I'm going to sing o-per-a in public."

"Then we're breaking up," I said glumly. "You do that and we're breaking up."

"No we're not."

I was impressed with her for a moment. She was finally arguing with me and I felt vindicated. Out the window I saw street people in ill-fitting clothes with tethered dogs and blankets and ruined lives and spotty, deathly drawn-out skin.

"Those people are free." I was whispering, like a little boy, into the window.

"Those people are slaves," said Suzanne in a very certain voice. "Slaves to the mechanism, Jarod. Just copies."

✳ ✳ ✳

I like this story. I want to publish this story. But I am not a publisher, I don't have an agent, and no one, not even my family, will take calls from me anymore. I am standing here, a solitary and lonely thirty-something man, dreaming of a publishing house which likes this type of thing. I mean they all say they like this type of thing (or, so I'm told by Maury)—this different type of writing and are looking for a reprieve from historical romance and need a young male voice to counter all the chick lit—but do they do anything about this? (Tut-tut from the Maurster! I can just see him flipping through *Publishers Weekly*, passing judgment on so-called "writers," crossing and uncrossing his feet in boredom.)

So I forget it, I put it down.

The phone pulses like a heartbeat. I click again.

It's Sinclair. I know right away because Sinclair is trying to sound cool and calm and in control and he hasn't yet said a word, but I know Sinclair and I know his way of being silent. I know he is planning his campaign of control and the thing about Sinclair is that he is just like me: thin and ugly, or handsome depending on your viewpoint. He is just like me, except he has a job, a plan even, power and money.

"I have film work for you, Jarod. I've pencilled you in for fire watch so dress warm cause it's going to be pissing down all day. Call time is five A.M."

I hate the phone. I hang up. Stare at the state of my room and throw a temper tantrum about the fact that I have about three hundred things on the go and none are ever likely to be finished. Plus, this will be a night shoot: dark, pissing down cats and dogs. Cold as hell.

SEVEN

I set the alarm for three and get up the next morning with an ulcer in my mouth because I forgot to brush my teeth. Because I don't have any money, I have to walk all the way to The Group Inc., which is located five miles away on the east end of Toronto. While I walk the two hours it takes to get there and plot how I'm going to keep this lack of bus fare secret from Adrieneese, I try to forget that I have put on the pants which have a hole eaten in the left pocket. I plot and scheme how I'm going to interview Mr. Jacob and get an advance on this film paycheque so that I can eat something, because it's been a plate of fries and ketchup and that's all for a week.

As soon as I see Sinclair in the camera room of the

production company I ask for his cellphone. I ask him if he wants a coffee so that I can go in the back and raid the fridge of all the cans of Coke and Five Alive and escape from the chore of loading heavy equipment into the back of the van. Then I will find a bathroom stall and try to call Mr. Jacob to finish this goddamned press release I am writing. Waiting in the loading bay while the rest of the lackeys haul camera equipment into the cube van, I dial my home number and find that Mr. Jacob has just called and left a number where I can reach him at the production company in Atlanta.

"One more call, Sinclair?"

"Yeah," smiles Sinclair, very elegant in his new Holt Renfrew duds. He is very reluctant to lift or actually touch anything. "After all, what's *five dollars a minute*, Jarod?" He hands me the phone again, smiles. I want to tell him that though he's younger than me, he's like a stepfather to me. Or a brother. But I don't want to offend my employer. So I remain silent.

The other film lackeys stare with contempt at me as I sit with my feet up on the passenger side in the cube van and claw toe jam out of my big toe with a pair of scissors and scratch down interview quotations on my the back of a call sheet. I keep going, chatting away with Mr. Jacob in the hurtling cube van driving to the cola shoot in Toronto.

Finally one of them cannot take it anymore.

"Who you talking to? Your girlfriend?"

I put my hand over the receiver. "Leonard Jacob. Commercial film director."

"Yeah right."

I don't say anything. Not because I am smart but because

the music is turned up in the van to drown me out.

EIGHT

I work all night in my crummy room on Shaw Street writing the press release for the animation company. When I am done I spot an envelope with a dated short story in it and I lie on my little futon and lick stamps on envelopes to journals that have not yet had the privilege of seeing my work. The next morning I get picked up at 6 A.M. by Sinclair in his white Jimmy and he asks me if I'm going airmail or surface mail as he peels a book of stamps from my shirt. He then tells me politely that I should brush my teeth and I feel like hell knowing that it has been two or three days at least.

NINE

When I'm back home I fall asleep on the spot with a chocolate bar in my mouth, which melts into the pillow.
    Phone rings again.
    "Is this Jarod Palmer?"
    "Maybe."
    "Jarod Palmer this is Visa calling how are you today?"
    "I'm not paying you back!" I scream just as Adrieneese

arrives at my door. She's wearing corduroy pants, the red corduroy pants I don't like much and she's delicately peeling a banana. She comes up, puts fruit in the bowl beside the fridge, washes down the counter and takes me down the hall with her to my bedroom. She lies beside me and I can barely keep my eyes open.

"Go to sleep with me, Adrieneese."

"Ay canno sleep."

"Hold my hand and close your eyes."

I begin to nod off, but I open my eyes. There are two large black marbles blinking.

"Ay canno sleep."

I get up with Adrieneese, pour the girl a glass of water and go back to bed with her taking up most of the room on the futon.

The next morning Adrieneese is grunting so loud in her dreams the entire world might as well know about it. I don't mind at all because the girl is stoked up, fiery red, like an oven in my bed.

But I cannot sleep so I run to the bathroom and piss. I then sit at the table in the kitchen and chew on a piece of orange. When the girl that boards down the hall walks into the bathroom I smile at her and she glares at me. I realize, too late, that I am eating her bag of oranges and that I don't actually have any oranges. I go back to my room, but Adrieneese is still grunting and groaning in her sleep like there is no tomorrow.

TEN

I work a few more times for the film company and have a little money to keep Adrieneese off my tail. I'm trying to save money to pay off debts, and pay back my Bay card so that I won't have to explain why I don't answer the phone. In Adrieneese's world, job plus money equals upgraded living quarters. In my world, job plus money equals comfort and if I get too comfortable I won't finish the Lana Banana novel. Ever. But who could I explain that to on a bus? Who could I explain that to anywhere?

So I take a job on a night shoot on a bank commercial that is being filmed on a closed-off stretch of highway outside the Toronto Zoo. The shoot is cold and rainy and I am given the job of holding the towel for the actress who is standing in the rain holding a cellphone while cradling a little girl in her bosom. I am yelled at by the assistant director because I am looking up at the towers marvelling how high they are and how hellish cold the rain is that is falling down over everyone.

It's the second day of the night shoot and I'm tired of listening to one of the production assistants I have secretly dubbed "the Dark Man" because he is short, speaks with a frog's croak and tells me his father owned a funeral home. He is relieved, though not inspired, to be working. He tells me that when he was ten or eleven he was working in the funeral home and had to do some "carpentry work" on a man who jumped off a bridge. He says that when people jump off bridges, they land on their feet and their legs get jammed up inside their bodies and have to be pulled back out with a huge set of tongs. I feel ill hearing this, so I try to stay away from the Dark Man and offer to get him coffees from the craft truck.

At the end of the shoot I am given the task of picking up pop bottles on the shoulder of the expressway which is fine because it gives me the opportunity for a little peace and to get away from the oppressive glares of the Dark Man. When they open up the highway I am retrieving pylons from the side of the road. Trails of cars come whistling past me making my hair fly away. My face turns white and I feel my heartbeat. I'm wet, splashed on, cold and miserable. My heart pulses like a telephone that pulses to let you know you have many, many messages.

The production manager, not Sinclair, smiles through the truck window as he pulls away and tells me that what just happened—while I was standing with my heart in my throat and my hair all blown against my face—was a wakeup call. Then, because he's a decent sort he puts the car in park, gets out, and tells me not to work so close to the road.

The boss tells me I should go home and get some sleep, so one of the film peons drives me home. I fall asleep in my small room that looks like a windstorm blew in from the hallway.

ELEVEN

Adrieneese wants me to meet her mother Eva the next day and so we go to her home in a huge complex that looks like a grey communist block at the top of Yonge and Steeles. It smells in the foyer of every kind of food: a peanutty smell, a garlic smell, a burned onion smell... I am crammed in the elevator with a whole crowd of Caribbean people with Adrieneese and her mother, who laughs once or twice but then gets silent as we all watch the elevator lights as we go up. When we open the apartment door, a fat calico cat scuttles down the corridors and sniffs at all the other people's doors and Adrieneese prods me to go get him.

Adrieneese has a mentally challenged sister, Maria, who lives with her mother and sometimes Maria and I get on better than me and Adrieneese. I am certain this is because Maria laughs at everything I say and I don't have to be careful with what I say around her like I do Adrieneese.

Adrieneese's mother is a nice lady and she showers me with little gifts of sweetbreads and stories. I like Ade's mother okay, though there is something about her that makes me want to get away from her as well. I'm not sure if it is the way that Adrieneese still calls her "Momee" or the way that she doesn't really listen to what Maria is saying, which, when the girl is constantly complaining about all her boyfriends, is usually pretty funny. However I know that I am just a visitor, not a caretaker, and I don't have to clean up after Maria or get her ready for work or bathe her like Eva does.

On the way back in the bus Adrieneese and I hold hands and I want to ask her why sometimes it's a little tense between us when we eat together, and why, when I ask her a question she always finds a way to talk about something else. We kiss, she tells me she loves me and tells me that when she says she *love you* she means it. She squeezes my cheeks together. "Yarud, chou make me crazy, chou naw?"

Afterwards I leave Ade cycling off somewhere and hit the bar for a beer and to watch the Blue Jays game on TV. Where I live it's all Portuguese people and fancy restaurants and people with cellphones and grungy bars where they look like they're plotting to kill someone and put them in the freezer till the end of the night. I like these bars a little because they scare me and it feels good to be anonymous when you're in the middle of seventy-five different projects—even better when you don't have to explain yourself to anyone.

I go into the bar, order a veal sandwich, and observe as people eye all six feet of me hunched over a fatty sandwich, which drips tomato sauce and olives onto the floor. I watch the game on the big screen: Blue Jays–Twins, whatever. One beer is three beers and I'm home lying in my bed, feeling a little numb rubbing my teeth, which lately are sore.

TWELVE

Phone rings and I answer it.

"Jarod P."

"Elliott?"

"How is it going?" I sense earnestness. A need. I look at the phone. Christ, I've just gotten home.

"I'm okay, Elliott. Surviving, barely."

"Can't talk for long. I'm out the door in two minutes. With studio people."

"That's cool, Elliott." I switch ears and unstick some crud

from my coffee mug. A year ago Elliott and all of his fantastic connections would have impressed me. Now it's the reverse. I shudder at the thought of a room full of attractive but thin, self-aware creatures rabbiting away on cellphones.

"I am at home, Elliott. I'm waiting for Adrieneese."

"The girl is not right for you. One day you will have your pick of them."

"I'm in fucking love with her, Elliott."

"We need to get together. I feel the need to connect."

I close my eyes. In my mind I think, *Phase this man out!*

"Pencil in January. You and I will go to a shooting range. We will fire rounds into a deer or cow carcass. How does that sound?"

"I'll have to pass on that, Elliott."

"Why don't we go skiing this winter? At a very good resort in the Laurentians. I will teach you the finer points of snowboarding."

"I have bad knees, Elliott. And no winter clothes."

"I'll lend them to you."

"I have a phobia of falling asleep in the outdoors."

"What?"

"As a child I saw my cat freeze on the doorstep of our house."

"We need to get away. I need to continue developing you."

"Gotta go, Elliott." I hesitate just slightly. I hang up. I stare at the receiver as if it will come alive on the spot. It does—the phone rings again. Crap and bloody damn. I pick it up.

"You are having reservations? About the snowboarding? We don't have to go. We can just sit in the lodge and nurse hot toddies. Plumb the depths of our remorse."

"Goodbye forever, Elliott." I slam down the phone.

If only this were true. The spectre of Elliott will never go, he is a horrible psychic ghost at the window, permanently tapping away after me.

THIRTEEN

The phone rings and rings and rings.

FOURTEEN

Realization, in the bath, staring at a cobweb above my head and the mouse shit and tiny spiders that live there as well: the Lana Banana novel has been abandoned. I will return to it, and I must return to it within the next month or I will lose all the momentum I have gained. I will return to it but first I need to explain to this man, this beast, this *creatura* that he must find a way to survive in the world without me.

✳ TAKING THE STAIRS: BEFORE LANA ✳

I have written three novels so far, twenty short stories, articles, press releases, book reviews, feature articles, screenplays, proposals, and plenty of acrimonious email to a woman who spurned me and still, I live breathe, and shit in obscurity.

I'm thirty-two now. Too thin for my own good, more unfriendly than ever and I exist in a city I hate. As we speak I am being courted by film people to write stories they think are original and yet which the village simpleton could tell you, in two lines, are not. Stories about aging movie stars brought back from the past, comedic tales of seventies excess, television pilots which make studio executives piles of money and which confine babies and children under ten to nannies and high chairs which they sit in and cry in when touched by human hands, struggle when held, because they are mesmerized by junk, fed junk, sold junk by morons with expense accounts.

✳ ✳ ✳

FIFTEEN

The phone rings again. I assume that it is Adrieneese but it is not Adrieneese at all. It is her mother.

"Yarud, where is my baby girl?"

"I haven't seen here in a couple days, Eva."

"Chu naw I am really worry about her. I have some tax problem and now I am hearing that her father is suing me because he says I owe hin money because I was with Jerry for three years. I need her to help me wit son legal documents, Yarud, if chu don't mine."

"Does Adrieneese know about the lawsuit?"

"Trus me, she know. You no know my baby girls jus yet, she know everything about her father. He is such a chit. *Rompe pelota. Ciao* Yarud."

"Bye Eva."

For a split second I ponder telling Eva about the Lana Banana novel, explain that I am trying *to finish* the Lana Banana novel, but then I think: why burden Eva with this? I can imagine Eva, in her slightly too-tight pants, with her expending waistband, sitting on her sofa, with her tax papers and law documents spread out before her. Head in hands. Lana Banana novel? I see. I see. *Muy bien. Muy feliz.* Eyes like slits and a slight hissing. *Nada argenté, no?*

Adrieneese arrives at my door and she is a beauty like you never saw in your life. She isn't picture perfect but she's a ladybug all right standing there in her red pants and her shirt with flowers and spots all over it. She has gifts of sweets and vegetables. She is smiling because she is happy and I've never felt like I loved anyone as much as I love Adrieneese, especially right at this moment. You can imagine that I am losing my mind, just to feel in the presence of this woman. How can I finish my Lana Banana novel when I am in the middle of life with her?

We cook some vegetarian dish that night and I spoon it

into Adrieneese's mouth and as much as I hate the idea of couples who do this, I still do it. Why? Because I love this damned noisy *mujere*.

When we are in bed it is good.

"Oy me." Adrieneese takes my cheeks in her hands and she squeezes them together. "Yarud sometime I jus wanna eat all you."

SIXTEEN

In the morning I am happy to just be alive and feel lucky to have lived any of the life I have led. Everything for the next few days is fine. The various jobs, dishwashing, telemarketing, journalism—all work for which I get paid. Adrieneese and I seem fine, though she starts telling me that she is interested in making films and wants to make them with me. I am so happy and overjoyed that she has said this to me that I tell her that we will do this as soon as I have published my first novel, the Lana Banana novel. Adrieneese groans at the mess on the floor and tidies up. Her face is red, it actually trembles and she looks at me and tells me that she isn't interested in waiting for me to finish the book or in being my personal secretary.

SEVENTEEN

Adrieneese and me are fine and living on vegetarian food and french fries, which we eat lots of at the local diner. Adrieneese is heavily into charitable concerns and likes to help out people in need and drags me out to various charity functions. I am told to sit there and take money, but I mostly scowl and crease the paper tablecloth with my fingers.

Adrieneese tells me I am lazy and spoiled, and while she'll never admit that she's the jealous type, she will leave me if she hears I am interested in another girl. She talks about films she wants to make and travelling she wants to do, and shows me ten or fifteen pages of a screenplay she has written. When I read it I can't believe how good it is. I tell her this and she tells me in turn that *she knows*. I feel slightly hurt by this because I can see she is irritated by me, so at this point the old Jarod comes out. It's the restless Jarod, the little bitch inside me.

"I'm stagnating at this table. I should be at home writing."

"Salis."

There is a wave of a hand and I am dispatched. I know that I will pay for this later but I also know enough about Adrieneese that if I start whining and looking guilty around the table things will be worse for me when she gets home. So instead of going home and writing, I go to my favourite Portuguese bar and eat *tosta mista* like I have been starving for three days. I sip beer, go home and don't answer the phone when it rings.

However, when I do check the messages it is not my beloved Adrieneese. It is an agency telling me that they have a four-day telemarketing assignment, which pays the princely sum of eight dollars an hour.

EIGHTEEN

I take the job again to satisfy Adrieneese and my own self because I hate the idea of having no money more than anything in the world. Adrieneese says she is proud of me because "eight dollar an hour ees better than a kick in the ass," but there is something in the way that Adrieneese is with me lately that makes me begin to feel like we are no longer as much an item as we used to be. She is sick of having to lend money to me and tell me what I am doing wrong in my life. I won't even mention *the book*.

I am immediately tense when I arrive in the small room full of computers and headphones and one highly self-important man in a suit throws me a script for telemarketing. I am a little annoyed when they put me in the room with a lonely, strange woman with a hood over her head. Her Walkman blares as she waits to make a call and I realize that I have been sectioned off with her. Everyone else in the large, well-lit room chatters away with one another amiably.

Then the strange-looking woman with the hood over her head pulls back her earphones and announces in a deep but resentful voice that she is a fiction writer, too. When the evening is over and I have made my twenty-five dollars, all the happy people crowd around the elevator on the fourteenth floor waiting to take it down. While I wait with them I begin to feel like I am being stared at. A panic attack sets in and so I don't take the elevator with any of them. I take the goddamn stairs.

NINETEEN

Adrieneese has been on this kick about being a writer for some time and for a girl that doesn't speak English too damn well, the girl notices things about people when she puts pen to paper. Her screenplay talks about the street kids who weave in and out of the back alleyways. The man in her screenplay is getting his haircut thinking about how he can buy a pistol so that he can kill himself with dignity when he is done telling all four of his daughters he loves them. I am in awe of her calm and easy ability to speak so many different tongues and I tell her she should be a teacher. She tells me that I should be a counsellor, a counsellor who dispenses unsolicited advice, and that one day she is going to be a writer—though not a neurotic basket case like me. *Uh huh.*

Instead of arguing with her or obsessing about the jobs in the classifieds that I am too lazy to apply for, I make tea and try to learn Spanish.

We sit at a table in the kitchen downstairs in the nice part of the house which the landlady will not admit is her own personal shrine but is her personal shrine and the fact of the matter is that she'd like it a whole lot if all the noisy tenants just stayed upstairs instead of sneaking downstairs during the day when she is off at work; after all how can six people rightly live in the rabbit warren which is upstairs? I cut apples on the table and Adrieneese has yogurt and she sits there and lists piles of Spanish nouns for me.

    My head in my hands.

    "*No se. No entiendes.*"

    A finger that points at me like a gun.

    "*Uno mas!*"

    My head in my hands.

    "*La vereda. La casa. Un banyo.*"

    A smile. First time in ages.

    "*Muy bien! Entiendes?*"

    A solemn reply. Uttered like a schoolboy. "*No pero entiendes un poco.*"

    "*Muy bien.*" Lips so wet they sting. I look at these lips and know I am a pig inside because I feel that they could be draining my root in the comfort of my stale futon but I cannot think this. This is unhealthy and I am desperately trying to remain healthy. Kind, pleasant and responsible. A kind man. A loving man.

    "*Parlez-vous français?*"

    "*Pourquoi?*"

    "*Parce que vous êtes fou et tres mal.*"

    I hate myself for knowing only a few words of several languages and for the fact that Adrieneese does not push me harder. If she pushed me harder we would probably be near perfect together. I could live up to my potential as a human being and she could communicate with me in a language which wasn't sex or food. But we are not near-perfect together, we are cracked and something tells me that Adrieneese still has a dose of the whore in her and that she is going to leave me for another eloquent young artist or writer.

Later in the evening Adrieneese is telling me that Momee is thinking about moving out of that flea-bitten skyscraper she lives up in northern Toronto and living with Adrieneese. I tell Adrieneese that just last week Adrieneese was telling me she wanted to live with me and there's no way all of us can live together: me, Adrieneese, her mother, her sister, the cat and the four other ingrates who live in this filthy rabbit warren with the Lana Banana novel and the seventy-five unfinished projects on the go. Adrieneese then tells me that Momee is thinking about putting down Cookie the cat, and thinking of the fat cat bothers me something terrible…

I cannot get the cat's fate out of my mind. Why should the cat die? What has the poor cat ever done wrong?

TWENTY

Since I have been so horny as of late, I dream of Heddy, who once visited my house in the Annapolis Valley while my parents were away, most probably in England. I never mention Heddy to Ade because she doesn't like the sound of her: *She zounds ly a snob, Yarud!* True. She's right (maybe).

Anyhow, Heddy was very good looking, and also very charming, except when she talked about food, which used to make me sick. (I don't miss that part at all. Alfredo sauce—the consistency, the texture of the noodles, for hours?)

Heddy liked my house because of the history. My mother has the lives of all us kids in volumes of photo albums, pictures on the walls, and there's a room upstairs devoted to athletic greatness, which was most evident in Rachel, the elusive fall-down beauty who gave my mother nervous fits most of her life. But my house is quite unspectacular (I am trying to capture this in the Lana Banana novel): plain, quiet, no television and that, I think, is what gave Heddy such a jolt when she first comes in.

She stands in the kitchen, surveying.

"I really thought you were a little rich boy, Jarod," she says there with the smell of cat pee in the carpet.

"Really?"

"Yeah. Everybody at university thinks you come from this big white mansion in town."

A pause. A look. "It is not something you deny," says Heddy, inspecting.

"True."

"It seems strange, don't you think?"

"What?"

"The way people are perceived to be."

This house where I grew up is like an apartment. An apartment with very little furniture.

"A large, lonely apartment, Jarod. What about Dr. Palmer?"

"He is the worst offender. He flies to the UK as often as he can: two, three times a year."

"What about your mom?"

"As you can see, she has absolutely no use for housecleaning.

She'd rather garden in the summer and sit and listen to an old lady sing war songs in a nursing home."

"And Rachel?" asks Heddy.

"Like me, very few high school friends."

"And George?"

"George is from here. He excels at being from here. If you whistle he will emerge from the stalks of cow corn with a golf ball and a couple of farm boys whom he has been shagging balls with."

Heddy sighs.

Heddy has a love-hate relationship with my brother, George, whom she has dubbed "the whistler" because he whistles at Heddy in the same way he communicates with the family dog but in a way that is so manic and terrible and funny that it makes Heddy cry with laughter. He is the class clown and has a needy energy about him and no one can do it as well as him, nor make you hate him as much as you do sometimes.

Upstairs we look at photo albums. George lined up against a wall with forty mischievous kids with hockey sticks and a shrunken man in glasses—Howie Meeker. Heddy is not interested in looking at pictures of George. Heddy looks at my sister, four years old with chocolate ice cream dripping down her chin.

She hands me the photo. "Even when Rachel was a child she looked clever and a little too smart for her own good, Jarod."

"Shit." I look at Heddy.

"What?"

"Why do you have to say these things?"

"It's true. She looks secretive in the photo, she looks cute as a button but like she's plotting something."

"Maybe it's because people like you have to make comments like that." I am surprised by myself, by my self-defensiveness.

"I don't know Jarod." She smiles.

I peel Heddy's blouse away from her shoulders and lay it on the quilt on George's childhood bed. The cats hop up and nimbly march over us. One meows...

I wake up, roll over. Try to sleep. Cannot. Dark hair down the back, face to wall. Oh Adrieneese, forgive me for this. I kiss her, but she is not impressed.

"Sleep, Yarud," she says, "we both need do sleep."

In the morning I wake up. She is gone. I panic, but not really. I just bound down the stairs, walk and walk and walk.

TWENTY-ONE

The phone rings and Adrieneese answers it.

"Hello?"

"Ade, it's me. I'm having an anxiety attack. My writing is shit." I stand at the grocery store and hold several parcels of food, which I intend to bring home and feast on with Adrieneese. I am feeling nervous as there is a line of surly Portuguese washerwomen waiting to use the payphone in the grocery store. A couple of cans of tuna drop onto the floor. I cradle the phone, pick up one of the cans and hand it to one of the dark-hooded, scowling Calibans behind me. I listen into the phone again.

"Yarud, chou are very talented. You were just telling me thees the other day."

"I'm certain of it," I whisper, "but why in hell's name doesn't anyone else know it?"

"Patience, Yarud."

"Goddamn it. How long do I have to wait, eh?"

Silence. "Yarud. Chu naw. Ay am going kome."

"What?"

"I no want this all the time, Yarud. Ay already have enough problems, eh? Why you gotta be this way, eh?"

Behind me one of the Portuguese washerwomen smiles as she can hear Adrieneese's voice getting louder.

I whine. "Aaaaaade!"

Now I'm in for it. More than five seconds of silence from Adrieneese is trouble with a capital T.

"*Rompe bola.* Chou may me crazee."

I stare at the assembled line of dark-hooded Portuguese washerwomen. They all look like the miserable old ladies from the *Giles* comic strips, except they don't speak English and come from the Azores. Okay, I step back. Time to leave. Out I go.

TWENTY-TWO

It's seven, eight in the morning and I've just had the most glorious sleep I've had since I was a pasty-white five year old and

Dar was taking care of me. I don't want to face the world. The phone is ringing, as ever. Still, something—guilt most likely though I don't know of what—compels me to pick it up. It's Elliott on the line.

"Good morning, Jarod. I've booked us in for golf at Don Valley at 8:30."

"Wrrrrrrrr…"

"You've been drinking haven't you, Jarod?"

"Wrrrrrrrr…"

"I've bought you a set of clubs. The finest design and craftsmanship."

"Wrrrrrrrr."

"I'll be there in thirty minutes."

I stumble out of bed, run the bath, fall asleep in it. If I stay asleep maybe Elliott will go away. I know that my biggest problem is this compulsion to do the nice thing and not establish boundaries with people and tell them when I really mean no. Elliott pounds away on the door downstairs and the landlady answers it.

When we're in the car I'm dozing, again.

"Remind me to add a cellphone to the to-do list, Jarod."

"Whaaaaat?"

"A cellphone you can keep on your person. And be on-call."

"That's the last thing I want, Elliott."

"Jarod, sooner or later you are going to have to recognize that if you want to make a living at writing for the film industry you are going to have to be accountable to people."

"You are the one who wants me to write for the film industry."

"You need money, Jarod."

"All I need is a word processor."

"And paper, stamps, a printer that works, literary contacts, a decent editor and money to survive—none of which you presently have."

TWENTY-THREE

When we play golf Elliott pairs me with a man who looks like an old pervert. His shrunken skin and wraparound sunglasses bother me. I cannot look at him in the eye without thinking he is an ancient queer lusting after me. I want to tell Elliott of this phobia but because I know Elliott would have a go at me in front of everybody, I remain silent and sullen. So I am paired with this old man, revolted by him, though he's eighty years old and can hit the ball miles farther than me.

When we all make our way back to the clubhouse, the old man invites Elliott and me to dine with him, which is fine, as I never turn down an opportunity to eat. Elliott and he start to get on well. They seem to know a few of the same people in the film business. It turns out this shrivelled old thing is a former studio executive and so I am left listening to these two cut salad and talk money. Then Elliott says to the old man that I am a burgeoning writer and the old man gives me a wan smile and asks me what I write. I tell him: I write about myself.

"Good for you," says the old man, and he puts his sunglasses back on. That's it for me; it's back to eating the vegetables in silence.

In the car on the way home I say, "Elliott, can I ask you something?"

"Absolutely," says Elliott.

"When you are in a crowded office building and you're late for a meeting, do you take the elevator or take the stairs?"

"Elevator, naturally," says Elliott.

"What if the stairs are faster?"

"The money men are always on the top floors. Why would you possibly want to take the stairs?"

TWENTY-FOUR

When I arrive back home I find that the landlady has left a note on my bed telling me that I will be receiving a bill from her carpenter as I left the water running in the bathtub and she had breakfast in her kitchen in the rain. She says that she understands that when I write I enter a different world and it is wonderful to be of that special variety of human being but would it be alright if I act like a normal human being and a responsible tenant.

I am filled with regret and embarrassment because my landlady is a kindred spirit and very good to talk to when things take turns for the worse. She has also confided in me some of her own misgivings about the way life goes sometimes and has taken to counselling people in the city who are overwhelmed with anxieties and problems—alcoholics, sex addicts, nutcases, the like. I go to bang on the door to apologize for being such an idiot but when I arrive there is another note on the door which reads: *No.*

Shame.

I realize now that I'm damned mad that I was born into this life one step behind everyone else. Though I am doing my best to put on a brave face, I cannot lift my head nor have a good laugh with friends anymore because I feel that we are in a state of being tricked. Our youth is being stolen from us by crooks who employ us in menial jobs (telesales, photocopying, press-release writing) till we are of no use and are corralled into a large barren field, like old cart horses, where we will be left alone to stare over the fence at the poor boyish fools working enthusiastically who do not yet know their seed will dry up, their boyish faces will wither and crack and their limbs will atrophy, turn to stone. And who is going to remember the work done by the enthusiastic peons? It will be filed away in boxes, stuck in landfills, left for seagulls and rats to clamber over.

Oh, Adrieneese!

TWENTY-FIVE

I tell my theory to Adrieneese in bed, which is the best place to discuss politics of any kind even if they are the body politic.

"Chou are cute, Yarud."

"Nawww."

"Jess. Chou are cute and chou are lucky."

"Why am I lucky?"

"I canno esplain. But I see girls looking at chou. Some guys don't ever get that."

"Yes. But I'm blind for one and don't see it in myself. And I do not aspire to be the broken twig in the raven's mouth."

"What?"

"Never mind."

"Why chou no happy today, eh?"

"What's to be happy about?"

"Today is beautiful day. We took pictures and sat in the park. Was beautiful."

I am getting tired of this. This need to be up, cheerful and upbeat.

"Why do you always go for white guys, Ade?" I say suddenly, overcome by a neurotic fear that I am about to be had. I am about to be usurped by a Spanish stud, most probably, a charming, creative one who doesn't have bad days like me.

Adrieneese tenses at this because she likes to be the one asking the questions and when I ask the questions they are part of some relentless interview.

"Because white boys always get sad and depressed, ly chou." Adrieneese gets tense again. "When ees good, ees good right?"

I kiss Adrieneese.

"Ees right."

Suddenly Adrieneese has a camera. She always has a camera. Even when she doesn't have a camera she has a camera in her mind and she might as well walk around with her thumb and finger at right angles because she is always framing things up like she has a camera.

"I wanna take a peeture of you. In those green pants tha chou wear."

"*Used to* wear."

"Whatever, put them on."

She laughs as I squeeze into them.

"Chou are getting fat."

The camera goes down on the bed. The pouting begins.

"When are we going to travel, Yarud?"

"When I publish my first novel."

She gives me that frozen look again. It's as if her face has been caught in some unimaginable state of disappointment.

"Just be patient, Adrieneese."

"I kam so patient, Yarud."

Oh yes, I catch myself. It is me that is not patient. Concern from Adrieneese, now. Yikes.

"Whay are chou crying, Yarud?"

I am not crying, I am yawning. I cannot be crying. I look deep into those black orbs in her head.

"I'm not crying, I'm yawning."

She has me pinched between her hands. Looking straight into me, through me.

"Chou break my heart, Yarud. Chou naw?"

TWENTY-SIX

In the morning the phone ring, ring, rings and I answer it.

"Jarod P."

"Elliott?"

"The room to the left of you. It is vacant, correct?"

I wipe sleep from my eye, and sleep from Adrieneese's eye. "You mean the room which houses my roommate?"

"Sure, yes."

"It is not vacant, Elliott. I live in a rabbit warren and have roommates, as you know."

"Damn."

"Why, Elliott?"

"I've summoned my lawyers. My wife and I are divorcing."

"Oh my god, Elliott."

"I'll be over in twenty minutes. I'll be bringing my suitcase."

"Elliott, you can't stay here," I whisper. "My room is the size of a dime and I'm also nearly falling to pieces."

"For a month or so, that's it."

"Elliott we'll both kill each other. I don't have space. My room is a box already. You'll be miserable with me. I'm very tempermental. In fact at times like this I imagine myself as a human matchstick. I might seem nice but Ade and I are on the rocks and right now and more than ever, I need my space."

The phone is dead.

Adrieneese is gone to the world as well. She is not snoring but she is as heavy as a sack of potatoes. Her black eyes are smiling, her skin is smooth. But she is red as a tomato. Snoozing away in peace. How does she manage this? I sit bolt upright. I shake her for all I'm worth.

"Get up, Ade. We gotta go."

Oh the guilt that comes with this as I rush away with Ade not yet dressed. But I've had this talk with Elliott before and I've been firm about this. I am a dummy in many ways but my own built-in bullshit detector tells me that it is not just my life, but his own that is crashing. I cannot, I *cannot* let him move in with me.

Two miserable souls in a room the size of a postage stamp is a dire situation. Elliott of course, half in the bag. Half dressed. Half a life wanting to be a full part of the equation. Still my heart breaks for him and that is the shit part of all this. I'm just trying to stay afloat myself and I can't let him sink us both.

TWENTY-SEVEN

At the Vietnamese restaurant Ade and I order a bowl of meat *something or other* and we try to share it as we both have birthday money and a flick to rent later on. I pick at the soupish mess and sip the weak tea. Ade is hungry and in it goes; next she spoons some of the raw eggy mess to me.

I pass the spoon back and stare at the door in horror imagining a large dented old-fashioned Rolls Royce slamming into the curb outside whilst a pallid, cadaverous madman with a cellphone glued to his ear stalks through the dive. I start to bang on my plate with my fork thinking about this. I can just imagine Elliott peering out the window of that car as I race down the streets in my pajamas. *Listen you fucking twit. Don't you understand? Fiction is dead. Write for me and I'll advance you five figures. Okay?*

I sip that warm tea. In my mind everything becomes dreamy. I can see myself:

I am young, handsome, kind, approachable. But I have an

ingratiating pallour like I've just come back from church or, worse, seminary college. I am seated in a room, at a round table with three other writer types. I am dressed well—*tailored* in that sort of Gap-clothes way. I have a laptop at hand.

I have healthy habits. I sip carrot juice, and weekend at the cottage of the in-laws, who have relegated me and my pleasant wife-to-be to the pool house. I make the bed, and dust instead of Hoover so I don't wake the neighbours. I beam pleasantly; I don't say rude or silly things.

There is an air of nervous expectation about me as if I am waiting to be told to clear off the plates at the end of dinner. Of the others in the room, one is male: slick, dark and very sharp. He writes a column about eating disorders for men in the *Globe and Mail*. Two are women. One is chesty, scratching in a notepad fastidiously. The other is an absolute oddity. She wears a hood, whispers to herself.

Elliott chairs this meeting of the minds:
Elliott: *Sitcom set down a manhole. Who's in?*
Tits Like Cannons: *What's the premise, Elliott?*
Elliott: *Does it matter?*
Slickster: *Dan Aykroyd in the lead role. I can get him.*
Whisperer: *Forget it. I pitched that idea in the late seventies. It was a third-rate clunker then. Then those fuckers at the Comedy Club stole my idea to throw that television set out the window. It's been open-mic nights for twenty-odd years.*
Elliott: *Shut up. You're contracted to write dialogue, not offer suggestions. Do you want to go back to filing books at Lichtman's where I found you? What do you think, Jarod?*
Me: *Manhole show?*
Elliott: *I'm paying you one thousand a week for content. I* own *you.*

Slickster: *Shit. Gotta go, Elliott. I've gotta panel a talk show at six. Digital or cable?*
Tits Like Cannons: *Network!!!*
Elliott: *Cancel, Rupert. You can't leave. We have a major studio ready to green light this.*
Whisperer: *Shades of 1979 all over again.*
Elliott: *Jarod, talk or take notes.*
Me (scrambling, shambling, whichever): *Certainly. Right away.*

The dream ends. I am staring at Adrieneese. And she is staring at her food.

TWENTY-EIGHT

When we get the bill from the waiter—a thin, balding Vietnamese man whose game-but-tired wife nurses their infant son in the front of the restaurant—I pocket the slip inside my coat. I find a handsome cache of Bay receipts, Visa slips and notes-to-self housed there. Adrieneese tells me it's silly to have all these things in my pocket but I resist and take a business card from the man, Thon Nuac, as well.

When we get home I finally relent to the pressure of getting rid of the junk in my pockets. I throw the mess into the garbage under the sink. I stay there in the kitchen as if it is a sanctuary. I'm not sure why. I feel like I just want to suck in air and hold it forever.

When I come back to my room and the movie Adrieneese is intent on watching, I cannot sit through the first half without going back to the kitchen, where I run the water and loiter about like a ghoul. Adrieneese is half asleep when I come back.

"Lay down, Yarud."

I do, slowly, pull the sleeping bag over us both. Adrieneese squeezes my hand.

"What you have in your hand?"

I show her the man's business card.

"Eet jus a card, Yarud. Throw it away."

"I know Ade, but he gave me this card. I like this card."

I look at Adrieneese and I swear that her face resembles a bright red plum.

"*Rompe pelota.* Chou are crazy, Yarud."

TWENTY-NINE

At four in the morning my dark Spanish horse is sprawled all over my bed and the phone rings and rings and rings.

THIRTY

When I lay in my bed, I dream. I dream of telemarketing, just because this is what is in my head and in my mind and ears.

There is a ringing, a buzzing like the phone which never stops. I am hunched over in a small cubicle. I am dead tired, I haven't shaved and my hair is parted in the middle if not sticking straight up. There is an overweight but attractive girl moaning on the phone in the cubicle beside me. I ignore her, just munch on chips or pop I have hoarded in the longish coat I wore to work because it is cold outside and I walk to work all year round. I keep calling, scared to look into the face of my boss, who is lurking, taking numbers down, calculating.

Hello sir! This is Mr. Palmer calling from The Medical Company of Toronto. THE MEDICAL COMPANY, SIR. I'VE BEEN ASKED TO CALL YOU. Sir, the great American Medical Company can give you a hearing test, which you clearly NEED.

Hang up.

Chatter from the moaning girl beside, who asks me if I have ever seen an American quarter. I don't look up, keep hamming on the phone.

Hello sir? I'm delighted to be calling you from the Great American Medical Company. We offer a premium discount card which you can use when you travel through all fifty of the United States, which will afford you peace of mind for only one dollar a day. You need to be secure in your healthcare! You know how expensive it can be. You do love your grandkids, right? You don't want them to die because you were too stingy to protect their long-term well being, do you?

I suddenly hate the girl beside me. Occasionally, she stares at me over the top of the cubicle with big cow eyes and it makes me slightly uncomfortable but horny. Occasionally she abandons the cubicle and takes to reclining in the recess of the window, sunning herself. She's Italian, with olive skin and a lazy, teasing charm—maybe this is my attraction to her.

I keep my head down while the lurker passes compiling a list of top performers, which I am at the top of, even though I hate this job. I have decided to come up with ways I can give the hearer bad vibes and impart in the drone of my voice that this is a crap job and a bad deal for them as well.

Hello sir, I'm delighted to be summoned to talk to you today, is one opening I have taken to. Another is, *Hello, sir?*

Hella? is another, stolen from the moaning Italian girl beside.

My personal favourite is: *Sir, please let me give you a moment of my time.*

I start to fall into the funk of the grub/bub voice. A grubbish, Annapolis Valley voice takes over and I am a comedian, a ten-cent head, a dullard—a loud voice in the office and I cannot help myself:

How yah doon, sir? My name is Jarod. I've been asked to give you a jingle to let you know about a little sumpin sumpin sumpin er udder we got goin' on aday. Not innerested? Come now fellah. I'm not gonna get the chance to give you a jingle again aday when I got a list a forty million people that me and the fine folk who populate this telemarketing office already gotta call. Why dontcha givver a try, guy? Why not givver a whirl, girl? No? Jeez, Louise. Hummina ding dang dongy donger. I'll tell you what, Mrs. Farrell, you are tigher n a-mouse's-hole-stretched-over-a-barrel. Not only is this med card some nice looking but it will save you money? Tell you what I'll eat the tax and deal you in: Two for four, tax in! What do you say? Did I mention millions have been spent? Millions more will be spent...

Then the worst thing that could ever happen happens. A

bad part of me takes over and I start to sell like all get-out. I take the DVD player, which is top prize on the floor of gifts stacked with *his and hers* watches, a cordless phone, steak knives, computer printer and so on. The boss tells me that I have a knack for selling and he asks me how I do it. I ruin it all by telling them I am a lonely person and have conversations with the people I sell to. I pretend they are my friends because I actually don't have any.

Then it's more moaning from the Italian girl beside me and I'm back at it again, hamming the phone line.

Hello sir. My name is Jarod.

Just a few dollars an hour. All for this. All so I can write at night for several hours and feel like I've accomplished something.

THIRTY-ONE

Adrieneese says she wants to move in with me but acts like she's about to leave. In her mind we'll all be happy in a kitchen with onions drying on the table and spices and yogurt and drinks of vodka and Momee and a cat or dog, too. It's not that we don't love each other... We do. And it's not that we don't love to do things together...

It's just that lately when we get together the both of us just stop doing anything and just *exist* together. It's so comfortable together sometimes that it's sickening. An inertia washes over us that is so strong that both of us feel like slugs, or something worse.

We lay in the dark, obsess about what we should be doing, then have sex in a slow and methodical way: fingers touch, kiss, press and ache in your whole body. This nakedness is as natural as getting up to make a bowl of soup, or to answer the door. The near-dead pleasure of screwing in silence disturbs me so much that I sink further into it.

Then Adrieneese is up suddenly and wants to be left alone while she takes some time to fuff about in her pajamas.

The girl is constantly on the move, in her study, shuffling papers, talking to you with that faraway voice as if she is lost under a pile of books. So I lure her to sit on the floor to watch television and some clever soul on an American talk show says actors are emotionally intelligent and not necessarily intellectually intelligent. I say that when I watch some actors' performances, I think they are dead inside and are faking everything, like they are going to a funeral of a friend they didn't know well. Ade is captivated by this expression "emotionally intelligent" as she sits with her legs at right angles then tells me to shut up as she stretches across the floor to grab a Spanish dictionary. Her hair is so black it may as well be coal. She says, scratching through the book, "What chou mean day inside?"

I tell her that when I see actors, all I can think of is they all seem to be caught up in *how* they want to say something, not *what* they want to say. The dramatics of it all drives me mad.

"Chou mean," says Adrieneese, "like chou, Yarud?"

THIRTY-TWO

Adrieneese is ignoring me so I pick up the phone to check my messages. My fear of the phone is so strong that I get a hard on. The worst part is I have a hard on as I stand beside Adrieneese, who is on the floor mesmerized by the television. I feel stupid, so I put a towel over it. I hold the phone and listen to the hesitancy of the breathing on the other end. Slowly the hard on goes and the towel falls.

Ade looks up with a wry smile as she stares at my stringy thing. I almost have the mind to lop it off to get rid of the curse of liking to fuck so much and the first message is from my mother. I'm standing there buck naked and listening to my mother ask me if I've been to church today.

When I listen to the second message, Elliott starts as he always starts, gravelly, like a cop addressing the mother of a murdered son: *Jarod P. It's Elliott.* It's as if this opening phrase communicates to me a secret psychic code: we belong to a certain unheralded and downtrodden sect called *men*. We need, dear boy, to talk about the greying of the flesh, the futility of life and never show too much emotion or happiness because we're men. We need to talk to one another until we depend on one another like drunks depend on the sight of another drunk in the room. We need to be friends till the liquor is poured and then we need to talk about the great, world-shattering screenplay we need to finish.

I want to tell Elliott that I think he will make a good director and what he wants to do in film everyone wants to do but so few have the talent to do well. I know this will go over well with Elliott, and he will be able to supply me with many reasons for it being so.

But I am also repulsed by the idea because I do not have faith in a drunk, power-hungry, stool pigeon who cannot park his car in his own garage without banging into it or racking up a thousand dollars' worth of parking tickets.

This is all part of the game—Elliott's chance to rant at a subservient, captive audience. And this is my chance to take a break from obsessing about Adrieneese.

Instead, Elliott says not to worry—he's back with his wife again and he's got another book for me to read. If it is another book like the *Confederacy of Dunces* about a flatulent, alienated bachelor dressed in a pirate uniform and hawking hot dogs in New Orleans, I will pull what is left out of my head and make him a hair sandwich.

But Elliott says it is a "first edition first novel by a local celebrity author." Although I feel a certain degree of repulsion and am convinced Elliott is just as cut off from the real world as I am, there is still enough of a glimmer of vanity in me that makes me think he is well connected in the film and television business and above all else, truly enamoured of my writing talent.

Despite how much I lambaste him, Elliott has been a surrogate father to me, though he is the last person I want to deal with. I would rather deal with the distracted, disinterested Spanish whore who is lying on the floor.

THIRTY-THREE

Ade lazily asks "why he want?" as she flicks away with the clicker and I tell her that while Elliott is less then charming to be around sometimes, he is one persistent son of a bitch. I continue in my neurotic and sad way to repeat that he is genuinely in love with writing and he is the only person I have ever met who likes it as much as he does. He appreciates the finer things in life—food, expensive clothing, cellphones, quill pens—and can afford to buy a piece of it all.

At this moment I want desperately to explain that there is a great deal of myth to writing, and the whole image of writing, and my being a male writer—horny, lonely, miserable—is ample proof of the old adage that writers should be read and not seen.

THIRTY-FOUR

The phone rings and I answer it.
"Palmer?"
"Yeah."
"It's Gregorio."
"Hey Shand, what's up?"
"It ees Gregorio Shandario and we are inviting youa toa de Rosedalio Golfario Coursario to dinner with your Esplanito momanion."

"Cut the faux Spanish accent, Greg. It sucks."

"Charming as ever I see."

When I get off the phone I have agreed to meet an old nemesis, Greg Shand, at his Bridle Path mansion with Adrieneese, who doesn't want to go. I am certain we have only been summoned to Shand's house because he and his new wife are bored and can't get down to the condo in Florida this weekend—or else their first, second and third choices for dinner dates have cancelled.

We dress in a hurry at my house and Ade is looking at me with lust in her eyes because we have just had a bath together and I have shaved, cut the hair on my neck, brushed my teeth for the first time in a week and still look like I can still knock 'em dead in a decent tailor-made Hong Kong suit.

"Why you no dress this way more?" Adrieneese is doing up my buttons.

"I would dress better if I had somewhere to go."

"Chou could go sonwhere like to a yob, Yarud."

I do up my laces.

"You don't understand, Adrieneese."

She says nothing, which is everything. She looks fine with her round Spanish ass in a tight, tasteful blouse. On the way there we stop off to see Momee at a flower shop where she is visiting a friend.

Eva pinches my cheeks just like Adrieneese.

"Chou look beautiful, Yarud. Wear are chou going?"

"To a party," says Adrieneese.

"A Bridle Path party," I interject.

Eva just smiles and I don't understand.

Later in the car Adrieneese tells me she is nervous about going to a party with people as rich as the Shands. She tells me Eva used to clean the house of a family in Rosedale, and then I begin to understand.

Greg Shand has a nice Greek wife with a perma-grin, a perma-tan and legs that could crack walnuts. She smiles at everyone but says nothing, and I know immediately that conversation is going to be hell with her. Then Shand is all over Adrieneese.

He pours her a drink. "I hear Spanish people have passion but little reason."

"Can I eat thees?" asks Adrieneese with a piece of chicken in her mouth.

THIRTY-FIVE

Adrieneese flirts with Shand in that way that Shand is always able to win the attention of women. For a short time, I am jealous. I stand there like a dolt and try to say things to the Greek who is good at saying nothing and smiling but seems like she could easily bite the arm off an armchair if there weren't "very important" people here.

There are waiters at this posh indoor party, mainly Filipino and Spanish, carrying trays of hors d'oeuvres with clammy shrimps and bacon rolls and salmon eggs and lobster bits. They are very tasty and the booze flows freely and generously. Adrieneese holds herself well talking to Shand while sitting on a leather sofa that nearly sinks to the ground. They talk of Brazil where Ade used to live with this blond tennis player she met while travelling, and how she had to watch him play tennis for days on end.

This of course has Shand in a tizzy—leaning forward in the chair and throwing his hands about—because he loves to play tennis and wonders whether this tennis player was on the Brazilian circuit. Adrieneese tells Shand the only circuit he was on was the short circuit because he had a bad temper and was known to throw temper tantrums just because he had corns on his feet that gave him terrible pains. Adrieneese has another shrimp and informs Shand that this tennis player had the *hot blood of a Brazilian man* in him, something she was never going to find in a Canadian man—let alone a Canadian man who went to private school and had a Filipino nanny wipe his bum for him.

Shand loves this kind of banter, so encourages it by telling her Spanish people have the short term down just fine but lack in long-term consistency. Adrieneese laughs while the Greek girl and me break crackers and have nothing much to say to one another.

When we get out of the Range Rover that drives us back down the Bayview extension and hurtles past the giant graveyard that is Rosedale, Adrieneese tells me that she never wants to see Shand again.

"He's not so bad," I reply.
"He hast never struggle, Yarud."
"You don't know that."
"I don't wan to know eet."

When we get ready for bed, I slip on my old uni shirt, a personal favourite like the green pants. Adrieneese is stepping out of her dress. She scowls:
"Not that shirt, Yarud. I hate it."
"I wore this shirt in university, Ade."
"Essactly, Yarud."

THIRTY-SIX

Sometimes when I meet the rest of the poor scribblers in my Toronto writing circle, who dream of getting paid for writing, I feel lucky to have met Elliott.

I want to tell them that some fortunate thing will happen in five to ten years if they keep at it and accept that most of what they are frantic and passionate about is simply a loose, stringy trail of unpublishable shite.

And while it is nice to have a patron of sorts, nice to have the attention of someone who somewhat appreciates what you do, surely all people who write (and are published) still stay the same: their minds are still hostage to the curse of writing, no?

But more importantly, I have come to view Elliott as not completely honourable company: he fails at a small but vital designation, which I term *the inside touch*. This is something my own shy, retiring dad has in abundance—a kindness, an awareness best explained in terms of reading a story to a child:

✳ THE INSIDE TOUCH (AN EXPLANATION, SORT OF) ✳

Those who do not posses the inside touch simply take the child's book, see it as a burden of adulthood and read the story with little emphasis. They answer a minimum of questions about the story, kiss the child, flick on the fairytale music and hit the lights, good night.

Those who possess the inside touch are able to understand that Washing Bug Lexxie and Black Cat Wintersinko are equal members and participants in the story of Lucy and Jeremy's *Big Trip to the Zoo*, even though the author forgot to write them in or add them to the illustrations.

They are still there, sitting in the window as cats, or tail-wagging dogs, or spiders dangling from the ceiling. They are there when pointed out by the child, equally as Lucy and Jeremy are there in the illustrations.

Washing Bug Lexxie and Black Cat Wintersinko need to be there for the child's imagination to develop. They are the code words to an understanding between child and parent that parent(s) will always be there to support and love them.

Washing Bug Lexxie and Black Cat Wintersinko are as equal and important to the child as a Grandma sitting on a couch with a pair of knitting needles teaching the child how to purl and add a stitch.

✳ ✳ ✳

How then to explain this to someone like Elliott, who has the attention span of a drunk? How to explain this to someone who believes in something called a story pitch? A character arc. A sound bite.

THIRTY-SEVEN

Just as I'm rushing to tell Ade how I'm going to get a job after I sell off the pile of film stock I have in the fridge, and how we're going to start eating out at restaurants every night for two weeks, I enter the kitchen. There are three little surprises on the table waiting for me.

The first two surprises are mail. The first package is a story rejected from a big Canadian magazine. It has a personal note, which gives me some hope. Can this mean there are actually people staffing these offices? After all, Maury has assured me in previous epic-but-deadening phone conversations that this particular editor with this particular magazine discovered more than one famous female international writer in his day. I scrutinize the scratchy handwriting and make out this recommendation:

> Your story reminded me of some dealings I have had with people in the film business. I found the story quite silly in spots, funny in others. Unfortunately we cannot publish this as we are in a tight fix with short fiction at the moment, but we wish you the best placing it elsewhere. Please understand that we get over two thousand short story submissions a year.

P.S. The dialogue is sharp. Have you considered writing screenplays?

Straight into the garbage. But then I hesitate. What if this is as good as it gets? At least this rejection slip was written on. I have proof of something that I have at least accomplished. It is a written-down, *signed* rejection.

When I am a hunched-over, miserable, old Uncle Jarod with my nephews and nieces, damned if I will acknowledge any memory of Black Cat Wintersinko or Washing Bug Lexxie! I can at least unfold this from my wallet and throw it out at my nephew or niece while visiting on obligations by brother or sister to have me over the Christmas holidays. With this tattered sheet of paper I have proof that I have at least had a go at something in my life…

The second piece of mail is a notice from a minor little magazine, to which I submitted to tease the editor. The note says:

> *Your story has been accepted to Thornhill's best niche e-zine, which caters to the poetry and science-fiction community. With a daily email list numbering over 210, your short story will be emailed in the coming weeks. Unfortunately due to our small size we have to pay in subscriptions. Please feel encouraged to know that you have been added to our email list and you are also entitled to a 20% discount to purchase our year-end anthology, which unfortunately, your short did not quite make.*

The third surprise is a short note, pinned to a bottle of wine.

*I'm sorry Jarod.
I cannot stay with you.*

—*Adrieneese*

I collapse. What else. I read the story.

THIRTY-EIGHT

✷ TALENT BY JAROD PALMER ✷

"The name's Mike," the young man said hesitantly, extending his hand to the production manager and shaking it. "Mike Allen. And I'm very happy to have been offered a position on this shoot."

A heavy-set man wearing dark jeans peered up from a nest of wires and watched Mike suspiciously, while one of the wardrobe production assistants, a girl in pigtails and a dark ball cap, bit slowly into an apple. Mike looked around, regretting that he had spoken with such a loud voice.

"Okay, Mike," said the production manager, with a faintly condescending tone, "let's make it official, since it's your first day." He waved his arms upwards, in a grand sweeping motion. "On behalf of the crew of this shoot: Welcome aboard." The production manager promptly tapped his pen against his clipboard, and stared at Mike in an agitated manner.

"Catering is ready in five," the locations manager roared, hands to mouth.

"These are the kind of shoots I like," Mike whispered to the cameraman who was fiddling with the focus button on the camera lens. "I especially like it when the Bravi Company caters them. Those guys really know their food."

"They're cheap," grunted the cameraman, adding a little deliberately, "Can I get a blue gel and a white balance for this shot, please?"

While Mike crouched down and sorted through the packed-up bags of wires and A/C adapters, all he could think was how lucky he was that his phone had rung that morning and he had been called to fill in as an assistant cameraman, even though he had very little experience in the field. Mike held the card up while the cameraman did a white balance check.

"Thanks," said the cameraman.

Mike handed him the blue gel. The cameraman frowned and pointed to the halogens.

"On the lights," he said. "Have you not done this before?"

During the break, Mike sat by himself at the craft tables and picked away at his plate of food. The ham was cold and burned, the salad was soggy and there was too much of it, and the bread plate had been picked clean of focaccia. He felt lonely—most of the crew was crowded around the young starlet of the shoot, a pretty, vain blond whose name was Jillian Carsperson.

The gaffer, a stocky guy with his jeans pulled tight at the waist, leaned into the table, one foot up on the chair. "That's the next step for you Jillian," he said. "Gettin' signed on with OMC. They'll get you the best leads and from there you can move on to more features."

"OMC," Jillian had a faraway look in her eyes as she said these words. Mike noticed that her gaze, like a camera slowly panning the room, drifted over to him. She looked at him for a moment then snatched her glance away.

"What I want is"—Mike detected a measure of the dramatic just then, as her head tilted to the side and her hands carved the air—"to get away from Toronto. I need to move south. That's the most important thing in this business, moving south. That's where all the real talent goes."

Just then the doors flew open and a crowd of extras came scrambling in. They fought over what was left of the stale bread, the marinated asparagus and the bean salad. They plunged their spoons deep into Jell-O moulds, hacked at the bloody carcass of beef, and twisted their forks round and round in the plates of pasta. They all sat together in one noisy cluster and cast contemptuous glances over towards the starlet before settling back into the frenzy of devouring their food. Mike sat by himself picking at his food. As he looked up he met the piercing gaze of a redheaded extra.

"Why you sittin there 'lone?" the redhead called waving her hand in a scooping motion towards him. "Come over here and sit with us."

For a second Mike was tempted. He did feel alienated where he was, though the idea of being seen with a crowd of extras seemed even more depressing. He looked around the room at the two options that lay before him: slumming with the noisy extras or sitting down with the crew circled around the starlet.

As Mike closed in upon the table holding his plastic plate out in front of him, he recognized one or two from the group. One was the locations manager who seemed to have an belligerent demeanour suggesting everything was slightly wrong; for example, the modest number of tables arranged in the dining room, the fact that the caterer had forgotten utensils for the food. She looked persistently at her clipboard, filed through papers, searched around for someone to direct. Another girl had frizzy brown hair, a blotchy complexion and a sort of embarrassed look on her face. She was laughing almost to the point of tears but stopped as soon as Mike arrived.

"Mind if I sit down?" he asked tentatively, pointing to an extra chair. The girl's expression froze.

"Here?" she asked. "Or on the floor?" She then broke into fits of hysterical laughter again.

As Mike sat down he realized that the frizzy-haired girl was a friend of the starlet's.

"The last shoot I was on," continued the starlet who was holding the frizzy girl's hand, "was a MOW for Alliance. The director wouldn't leave me alone. He had me in his trailer all the time talking about the character's *vulnerability*. How she'd been molested by her father and didn't trust men."

"So the director, he tried to molest you?" the gaffer asked, knees bending into the table.

"It's this business," Jill started, defensively, her voice

rising. "I don't care what anyone says, artistically or otherwise: it's all about sex."

There was a strange, uncomfortable silence and Mike felt that he shouldn't speak or look at anyone for some time. Suddenly the second assistant director arrived in the dining room.

"On set in five," he yelled as he adjusted his headphones.

The scene they were filming was a love scene between Jill's character and the lead male, John Jeffery Markham, also known as *JJM*. It appeared to Mike that John Jeffery Markham was a poised, professional actor, who took great care to prepare for his role. He behaved, it seemed, aloof to Jill. There was little chemistry between Jill and JJM and little chemistry between JJM and the crew. But he did have a great tan, between takes smoked cigarettes, and talked a great deal with his assistant, a pretty dark-haired girl who wore her hair in a ponytail. Jill was in a robe and fussed a great deal.

"Do we need absolutely everybody in here for this?" she asked.

"You." Jill pointed at Mike who was fiddling with the monitor to the camera. She was waving her hand toward him. "You don't need to be here, do you?" The director looked at the cameraman. The cameraman nodded back.

"This might take a few takes, Jillian," replied the director, tiredly.

JJM took off his robe first and got into the bed. It was a four-poster brass bed, covered in satiny blue sheets with white light slanting down from above. Mike couldn't help but notice that JJM was wearing a thong and his upper half was darker than his lower half, smeared with dark flesh tone. His upper body was also well-muscled, but he had short legs; his physique reminded Mike of a toddler. Jill let her robe fall to the floor and then got into the bed quickly. Mike looked down, embarrassed, but soon found his gaze shifting upwards.

"Like this," the director was working with the aid of the diagram. "Underneath the breast, cupping it and then move in on the nipple. But don't dwell on it, it doesn't look natural. That's the thing. Everything's got to look natural. Know what I mean, JJ?"

"Know whatcha mean," replied JJM, looking unimpressed.

"Alright. Set quiet." The director looked towards the AD. The AD's arm pointed skywards as he watched the director. The director nodded. "And rolling. Take one." The AD's hand chopped downwards in a broad sweep.

"Action."

Jill was wearing jeans, but was naked from the waist up. The camera was positioned overhead looking down and JJM began by kissing her stomach, above her belly button, then moving his hand over Jill's breasts. But his movements were too hurried.

"Cut," said the director. "Too fast, JJ. It's got to be more gentle." The director looked around. "Makeup!" he called. "Mist the forehead please, and please JJ, more gentle."

Jill leaned up, took a drag on a cigarette, undid the top of her jeans.

"I feel so bloated."

"And again," said the director, sighing. "Take two."

This time there was music in the background, a saxophone shrieking.

"Sexy, now," said the director. "Let's set the mood, Jillian."

There were more takes. Breast kissing. Forehead mopping. A close-up of hands, clenching, releasing. Longing looks, breaks, kissing. Mike noticed that the shots seemed rushed, out of sequence.

"Break," said the director, running his hands through his hair. He seemed irritated. "Take five, everybody, take five. Jee-sus Christ, Marty."

The AD looked bewildered.

The crew dispersed towards the coffee dispenser on the craft tables. Mike followed them.

"Not you," called the director.

Mike stood there for a moment while the director and the AD conversed. "I can't stand working with this guy, Marty. I mean it's like he's got one brain cell in his head. Where'd we get this guy, anyways?"

"MMD," replied the AD.

"He seems too familiar or something, Marty. I mean, there's just this kind of routineness about what he's doing, it's sort of... unsettling." The director paused.

"Think he's worked in porn?"

"MMD? Major Metro Darlings!" The AD thought for a moment. "Could be."

"I think he's worked in porn," replied the director in a dazed voice. The director thought for a moment. "Did you get a good look at his hands?"

The AD shook his head from side to side, slowly.

"He has a big fat wart on his knuckle, Marty, and the skin around it is all scaly and chafed."

The AD stood with his head angled back away from his body. "Rude," he said.

The director approached Mike.

"Tough shoot," said the director.

"Yeah," replied Mike, noting that the director had a strange, overly friendly tone in his voice.

"What do you think of the actors?"

"They're okay," said Mike.

"Mind if I take a look at your hands?" asked the director. Mike extended them.

"Go like this," said the director. He mimed the air like he was washing a window.

"Good," he said.

"Ever acted?" he asked.

"Not in film," replied Mike in an excited voice. "Community theatre, that kind of thing."

"Perfect," said the director.

"We can do this," said the director, looking at Marty. He looked at Mike, thought for a moment, then stared at his watch. "We should, you know, reconvene."

They shot for four more hours and then broke for the day. As the cast dispersed, JJM stood around the director and indicated that he wanted to talk. The director ignored him, at first.

"Sorry," he said, with a wave of the hand. "Unless it's related to today's work, I can't talk. We've got a schedule to meet here."

"This has been brewin' for quite some time," groaned JJM.

"Lookit," the director replied, his mouth pinched, "if it's related to today's shoot, then by all means let me know. But honestly, JJ, if this has been building up, the time to talk about this isn't now. It was two days ago, or a week ago—you can't just let things slide."

"I don't need this," said JJM shaking his head.

The director leaned into him. "Not in front of the crew, JJ," he cautioned.

"I don't need this," replied JJM.

"Talk to the producer then," said the director and he promptly glided away.

"Mike, Mike, Mike. Listen to me, a caressing motion, okay? Gentle, slowly like you're waxing a brand new car. Gently, gently, gently." Mike wiped the sweat from his forehead, and continued as he had before. "That's it. Cup the breast with your hand, then lean in to kiss it... Stop. Perfect." The director nodded up and down at the AD. "Okay. Take that outta here and let's prep for the shoot."

An assistant wheeled away the mannequin torso. "Where's Jillian?" the director asked.

"In makeup," said the AD.

"One take," the director said. "I'd like to do this in one take, Marty."

Jill took one last drag on her cigarette and stubbed it into the lid of a Coke can. She loosened the top button of her blouse, and stared at Mike.

"One take," called the director from afar. "Just one take if we can."

Jill looked at Mike shrewdly, and inhaled sharply, no smoke. "Let me see your hands," she said.

Mike showed her his hands, turned them over once or twice.

"You do have nice hands," she said in an impressed tone.

"One take," repeated the director.

"Have you ever considered hand modelling?" she asked.

"No," said Mike.

"Good money in it." Her eyes widened.

Jill placed his hand on her breast, readjusted herself where she lay on the bed, and the saxophone shrieked.

Mike did as he was instructed and the scene was recorded without difficulty in one take.

"Cut," said the director.

Jill looked at Mike afterwards. "You're good with your hands. Do you have an agent?"

"For what?"

"For making use of your talent. You have beautiful hands…"

"Mike," said Mike, quickly. "My name is Mike."

"Right," said Jill.

Mike felt awkward, but then he didn't so much. He felt like flailing his hands out in front of himself theatrically and

waving them about. He felt like flirting. With his hands.
The second AD handed him a pencil and pen.
"What's this for?" asked Mike.
"For accreditation," the second AD said.
Mike looked at the paper that said, *Talent: Hand model* ____.
"For if you want to get paid," repeated the AD.

Later in the shoot Mike had a certain lightness in his step. He dallied about the craft truck, and pleased himself by saying rude things to the redheaded girl and reminding the gaffer that his jeans were too tight. It felt good and he couldn't stop himself; the commentary just came like a polished oration he had never delivered. He found himself flipping through the glossy magazines with the agency people. He pointed at an anorexic model. "She looks like a stick with tits," he said.

"Very clever," said the agency man.

"Mike," said Mike, extending his hand.

"Do you have representation?" asked the agency man.

Then whilst sizing his hands up in front of his face like a director, Mike burned his right hand on one of the halogen lamps.

It wasn't a serious burn in the sense that he wouldn't ever be able to use his hand again, but the scar was dark and covered the back of his palm along his knuckles. His face went white.

Jill appeared puffy as she came out of the bathroom and had a look of need about her. She sized him up straight away with a consoling look, scrutinized his palms and pushed his hand away.

"God, how awful! What will you do now that you've squandered your only talent?"

* * *

THIRTY-NINE

I take the note, burn it, and drink what remaining alcohol there is in the house before hitting the bar, wearing the old uni T-shirt that I have not changed in days. I have an ashen feeling about me as if I have been summoned to jury duty and the first bar I walk into will be the Court of Truth. The judge has been waiting for me. He says stiffly and seriously that the *just fooling around* stage of my life is now over. Then he says: "You are now entering the *what good are you now?* stage of life."

I enter a murky-looking Portuguese bar, with scads of grim-faced, short men seated at small round tables munching on peanuts in round bowls. I prop myself on the stool and try not to stare at the bartender who is patient with me but tells me that the bar is a family place.

I feel relieved because I am sure this means that if I don't wish to converse with him in Portuguese then I can now set into the duty of drinking. The beers are on for half price and after a bit I chat with a startled local and tell him all about my life in Nova Scotia and the decisions I made about coming to Toronto to try to make a go of things. Everyone in the bar seems so nice, so friendly that I order round after round of drinks, drinks for everyone, and I confide in more than a few that I am in love with a Spanish whore who is great in bed, a moaner when she is sleeping.

I weave towards the door at the end of this production with the contents of my wallet spilling on the floor, including all my credit cards that have no credit on them. Somehow I get home and come to a slow but definite realization that I'd better not go there again. I have a bad feeling that I have done something very stupid: not paid for the bill and, perhaps, taken a swipe at someone. This fear is confirmed as I lay in bed and dream of sore hands and knees and the sound of a car driving away after I am dropped off at a bank machine that has no damned money in it.

At night the phone rings and rings and I lay in bed not wanting to answer it for fear that it is the police, or worse, the bartender. After some time, I go for it because in my heart of hearts I want it to be my Adrieneese or my mother saying they have both spoken to each other and they have made plans to reform me and repair the wrongdoing that we silly young souls have inflicted on one another.

I want to hear my mom tell me that I'm simply to be banned from writing anything ever again: I'm to spend the next four years as an English teacher in a foreign country, exiled from Adrieneese and my mom, till I pay everyone off. It is not my mother, of course, it is Elliott.

"You've been drinking, haven't you Jarod?"

How in Christ's name does the bastard know? Instead of hanging up, I give him my very best bits.

"Your cab is here, Elliott."

"What?"

"You are the drunk, bastard. I am just trying to get through the week."

"Call me at six, tomorrow." Click.

I do not.

FORTY

I am now walking the back alleyways of Toronto. The sun is sharp and hurts my eyes and my hair smells like the bar I may have been thrown out of. I am in a state of bliss, with a few peanut shells in my pockets to remind me that I've had dinner and breakfast as well. I have donned a long black coat, which gives me the look of a spectre in the window. My pants are a day dirtier and there is an element of security knowing that I look like a bum from the park and have resigned to acting like one.

In my mind I make up a little song. I sing it as I wander along the streets and it is a song I love to sing because it is a song for Elliott and it is a song for Adrieneese. I decide to sing it to the tune of Beethoven's *Ode to Joy*, not because I am pretentious but because it was on CBC when I got up and sat on the toilet with my head in my hands. One of the Portuguese washerwomen who inhabit this neighborhood catches the sight of me serene, hopeless, head turned to the sky. She scowls at me.

I sing, crackle:

Kindness, patience is a virtue
Has my Elliott left me alone for one day?
A simple act of goodness, well, kindness
That Spanish whore broke my heart today.

Oh, crikey. I start to cry. It feels okay, actually. I'll be okay.

FORTY-ONE

The library is ruled by Mrs. Ward—a kindly spinster of forty, rail-thin and neatly dressed—who views, I suspect, all snoring men and bag ladies as furtive writers plotting desperate assaults on the suggestion boxes into which they will cram a napkin with the title of their out-of-print book of poetry on it.

I, in my state of delirium, am in a fine mood. I lose myself in the periodicals, fashion magazines and immediately identify with whomever I am reading about: a major movie star, an athlete, both of whom I note had difficult pasts, were school delinquents suffering from autism, had broken arms, were largely ignored by their peers… Of course some ungodly talent has made them rich and famous beyond all get-out.

I approach the librarian, who is smug enough to smile. After assuring her that I am not a writer there to plug my own book or to ask her out on a date, I convince the old dear to put up with the various false starts, the memory loss, the head in hands, and she kindly and politely helps me get a movie ordered through the city library system.

FORTY-TWO

When I get home there are two messages from Elliott.

The first one is scratchy in tone, issued like a drill sergeant: "Meeting with BIG MAN AT NETWORK STUDIO about pilot idea." The second is: "MONEY INVOLVED."

FORTY-THREE

I am getting out of Elliott's car after some deliberate, slightly tense conversation we have just had at a local coffee shop, where he has insisted on paying for everything.

He says, "About your writing: you have the talent to go a long way. Mainly as a screenplay writer, because your structure is suspect but your dialogue is sharp and funny."

"Thank you for the advice, Elliott."

"Are you okay, Jarod?"

Is this a dream or reality? I do not know. I am just in the street, hungover or sober and I am not exactly sure if Elliott is real or imagined anymore.

FORTY-FOUR

The phone rings and it is Elliott.
"Jarod, can you paint?"
"Yes." I can do anything. I am still half asleep. I can write speeches. I can hammer on a typewriter. I can avoid the phone for days.
"Can you meet me in an hour?"
"Christ. Where, Elliott?"
"In an alleyway uptown."

I meet Elliott in an alleyway. I am patiently and appropriately attired in an old ball cap, my T-shirt and painting clothing as I assume the bastard is about to drive me to some upmarket Rosedale house and drop me off under a tree with a tarpaulin and gallons of paint. As always, Elliott is on his cell and has a boyish and stylish new haircut, though there is something of the cadaver about him as he totters down the street as if has been kicked in the shins by his wife. There are also two new yellow parking tickets stuck on the front windshield of his car, which sports a fresh dent.
"You are late," Elliott says.
We do not paint. We simply go to the bar and drink.

Elliott knows nothing of the Lana Banana novel. I tell him that I have been working on another short story.
"What is it, Jarod?" asks Elliott, staring from the base of the glass.
"Nothing, Elliott," I say. "An experiment, at best."

"Oh," says Elliott.

This bugs me so much, I can't stand it. I can't say why exactly. Perhaps it is the disinterest in the short story and the obsession with crappy screenplays. I stare at this man with foppish haircut, jeans—a cadaver with knock-knees.

"Elliott, I don't want to write screenplays. I want to write novels but I've been writing these short stories for years."

"There's no money in them, Jarod."

"I know that, Elliott."

"Then why do it, Jarod?"

"Because I love writing them, Elliott. They give me enormous pleasure."

"Good short stories take years and years of crafting, Jarod."

"I'm in no hurry, Elliott."

Elliott has a stare on him that could bore right through me. "You don't have the patience to write novels."

"That's the only thing I have, Elliott. Money is not the most important thing to me."

"Money can buy time. And purchase talent, greater than yours. Ditch the fucking lark and write for me."

"Never, Elliott."

"Jesus Christ you are one naive cunt."

I look at Elliott. He is killing me. He is a ghoul hammering at the window. I feel as if I am a captive slave and he has caught me with a book reading at candlelight trying to better myself. I ball my fist.

I do not hit him. But I would like to.

FORTY-FIVE

In the morning I am shuffling between skyscrapers in this fine city of Toronto, looking for an address of a building where I will nod and rush past the secretaries who will be polite to me even though I look like I have never seen a hairbrush in my life. I will disappear into the back and take a seat at a table by myself, and will lick envelopes with people in Accounts for the princely sum of ten dollars an hour. There, in the shadows of this corporate tomb, I will be able to revaluate my life in all its terrible pointlessness and gloom.

But before I can make it to the job or building, the powerful and paralyzing urge strikes to take a shit. But I cannot tolerate shitting in public washrooms. I try not to think about this as I go into the washroom and check underneath the stalls to see if there are any dirty old men waiting for me. I remember a friend who told me while he was on the john in a public washroom, a little Chinese head appeared underneath the door and said, *Suck your cock?* My imagination takes a further liberty as I near-explode thinking of a little hired man who rides a luge around the public washroom, stuffing himself under recently vacated stalls and fulfilling a debauched but occasionally profitable public service.

I clench my cheeks, and decide I must go home.

So I call the agency and tell them I have come down with a bad migraine and a bad case of nerves and an anxiety attack. They frown on this. Ominous things happen as I sit in the subway waiting for the damned thing to get going. In the silence I note that the noise as the door opens sounds like the first three notes from *Sesame Street*: *Sun—eee—day*.

As I sit, I notice the private miseries of the people who sit in the seats beside me: a woman with an absent expression and a tight pantsuit with a purse nailed to her lap. There is an Indian man watching me furtively while scouring the newspaper; a rapper and his woman, cornrows and braids. A Latino woman with pasty face, freckles. We are all waiting in silence in this barren, dead city. When the subway gets going, the conductor announces the next stop and I cannot help but notice that the low drone of his voice—*Ossington, next*—sounds like he is mocking the whole lot of us.

I shiver at the thought of this and picture a gargoyle with a sneering face descending from a vent in the subway ceiling, whispering: *Fools! Peons! Clowns! Terrible things will happen. Get out now! Get out while you can!*

FORTY-SIX

In the bar, Elliott orders two beers and takes out a sheet on which he has written an outline he has received from a promising source—a grip or gaffer on a television show. The story idea is about a footballer who comes out of retirement to play—one last time—in the 2090 World Cup. There are cyborgs and spaceships hovering about and the game is a championship game, a final. I tell Elliott that I like the idea but don't like that it is set in the future as I have no interest in sci-fi writing, don't think I could do it even if I tried.

Elliott tells me that I'll start to act more mature when I start to make money. He asks me if I want a coffee to sober up. I say no and he tells me that there is a simple thing for me to do but I have to act quickly and I don't have to paint anything but he has something else in mind to keep me occupied (and as near to him, and under his thumb, as possible).

I look at this man. Even though I am still young, I do not feel young. I am broke, wearing the same pants and shirt I wore at university. I stare at this cadaver, this *creatura*, still alive, just barely. Elliott explains that he is going to use his connections to make a feature film if I can bang out a screenplay for him for two thousand bucks. I look at the synopsis he hands me. I get canny and tell him I'll take the job but only if I get to write *my own* screenplay, *my own* topic. Elliott gets very somber and serious about this. He pauses and tells me that I am getting closer to being a more mature, developed human being.

FORTY-SEVEN

"Jarod P.!"

"Elliott?"

I hear noises in the background. A woman's hopeful voice, sounding as if she is just out the door. I keep listening. Exasperation and a deep groan, perhaps a dog being trod on. "Jarod. My stepson T.J. is having his thirteenth birthday party in three hours. They've invited everyone. His schoolmates, mother's friends and so on. They've made me master of ceremonies for the damned thing. Do you write speeches, Jarod?"

"No. Just make something up, Elliott."

"I can't write, Jarod. Christ, I've tried. Everything I write is so dull. I need your expertise on this one."

"What makes it dull?"

"I've devoted two pages to how T.J. used to run naked around the garden and piss in the rosebushes. I want T.J.'s grandmother to hate it. She thinks I compete with the child for his mother's attention and that I want to embarrass him in front of his friends."

"Maybe you are going to embarrass him in front of his friends."

"Nonsense. Plus, T.J.'s making a grand entrance with his new lacrosse gear and skateboard by showing off on the new ramp I had built in the backyard. This is after we tribute his life with a slideshow."

"That sounds like fun, Elliott."

"It's called wasting a young life."

"You're only young once, Elliott."

"Just fax me some pleasant-sounding copy and there's fifty dollars in it for you."

"I can't do that Elliott."

"You will."

FORTY-EIGHT

Elliott hangs up. Bastard.

In my mind I have this image of Elliott straggling across the surface of a rink, Maple Leaf Gardens, skating on his ankles while a spoiled boy in a ducktail haircut punches on his PalmPilot and skates rings around Elliott.

"Can't we just go, Elliott?"

"No we can't, for Christ sakes, go. It cost me a small fortune to rent this building and this has been written into the pre-nup. This is part of our bonding session. Now hold my effing hand and start talking."

FORTY-NINE

In the spirit of the good sex I imagine Elliott and his lovely wife Sharon have when the children are sent off to boarding school, the clothes that get thrown across the house when they see each other in a hopeful light, and the dog-fart stink that inhabits their room when their meek, nose-in-your-balls pooch creeps in to settle into one of Elliott's thrown get-ups, I decide to have a go at a speech.

I do two versions. One for Sharon, whom I attended a painting class with, at Elliott's beckoning, months before. She is charming, with a good sense of style—a lusty, hands-on-leg gal, though I shudder at what she might say if you were late, or ridiculed her son. Still, I like her easy, sexy way and especially the fact that Elliott told me she once stomped onto an American film set and announced: "Who do I gotta blow to get the job?" I like to talk to her when I get the chance, which is rarely; Elliott has seen Sharon's hand on my leg more times than he will admit noticing.

I hope Sharon's version will please her, whom I imagine at this particular moment to be forcing Elliott's balls into a small vice and smiling at him while turning it slowly, saying: *You better pay the goddamned rent here, Elliott, because you are not in my good books and I love my son!*

FIFTY

Sharon's version of Elliott's speech:

> *Hiya, kids. Welcome to T.J.'s birthday. Now if you would all take your seats at the picnic tables, I'll be able sneak out back. While I'm there, you may kindly take a moment to have a sip of your Roy Rogers' and then would you please stand and join me, as I return in fancy dress, to welcome Tyler James Doyle-Bale into the room. As a (step?)father it has been my pleasure to watch T.J. develop into a bright and promising lad who has a caring nature with women. As some of you may know he has also shown tremendous athletic promise in hockey, lacrosse and golf. To make the most of this ceremonious occasion, Sharon and I are pleased to let you know that T.J. will be joining some of*

you at the Toronto Boy's School in the fall. To celebrate this wonderful event, Sharon and I have asked your parents to let you all spend two weeks at summer camp north of the city with him.

Elliott's version:

Dear toe-heads and halfwits,

True, I've been blackmailed into roasting the little prick who buries my cigars in the garden, bawls on cue and has smoked half my bag of reefer. Touch my pot again and I'll lock you out of the house and tell your mother I know you're dipping your wick in that little cock-tease next door whom I've wanted to bang since I moved into your mother's house. Two things give me pleasure in being asked to roast the little weasel who steals your hockey cards and lifts your best jokes to use on girls. He's got a father he visits in Los Angeles twice a year and I've told that jerk to come out of rehab a month early to do time in the woods with the lot of you. Don't think I don't know you are at that Toronto reform school plotting to steal your brothers and sisters' share of the inheritance. I was there too, boys: if the drink doesn't get you, the first family Christmases after puberty will. Oh, and one more thing: the next time one of you laughs at the parking tickets on my car, I'll remind you that I could very well be your *father.*

FIFTY-ONE

I slide both versions into an envelope, seal it and leave it on my porch, tucked in behind the drainpipe for Elliott to collect. In the night I wake up thinking that I must be mad to have written such a horrible thing about a child I've never met, just heard about, in varying stages of praise and reproach, depending on how many parking tickets Elliott has had on his car windshield that day. When I get downstairs the damned envelope is gone and there is a replacement envelope with one crisp fifty-dollar bill in it.

When I come back up at 2 A.M. the phone is ringing. I do not answer it but cannot sleep all night so pick up the phone in shorts and no shirt. I catch myself in the mirror and see that I look less like a gangly stork and more like a pear with legs. Battling the depression that accompanies this, I take the message from Elliott. The message says, "Fucking genius, Jarod. Will show first speech to Sharon and go with speech number two."

FIFTY-TWO

All day for weeks on end I obsess about Sharon calmly showing up in front of my place in a rental van with all of Elliott's shit in it.

"You two are perfect for each other." I can just see her

wheeling him, passed out, snoring, in one of her old couches. "Mother always said Elliott needs a nursemaid, not a wife!"

I have a go at my fingernails just thinking about this. I am sure that at various stages of this wretched life I love Elliott just as much as I loathe the son of a bitch. I ponder having him read an old short story and convincing him to option it so that I have to do even less work. After all, why write a treatment or a screenplay when I've already banged out a story? I've already done the work for free, why not get paid for it?

Damn it. I throw myself under the table and read out loud a note attached to a story I had hidden from sight. I look at the note, kindly and meticulously written out. It reads:

> *This story is slightly too earnest in tone to be publishable. I would recommend that you buy one of our literary magazines in the future in order to have an idea of the kind of work that we publish. This is also a very old-fashioned style of writing and we are looking for fresh new writing.*
>
> *Of course what this means is highly impossible to specify and is very difficult for this magazine to define what new writing might be... I suggest you enroll in one of the creative writing classes being taught at the schools of continuing education and try and mentor with one of the...* (hobbyists!! ed. me) *who run these* (puppy mills!! ed. me).

I read further along and see I have scribbled further: *Oh bugger you hopeless little punter. Why don't we just make it simple for you?*

Unless you have some friends in the publishing business... save your postage!

FIFTY-THREE

I must escape from this, so I take the phone off the hook. I climb into bed again, remake it first so that it feels tight, secure, contained. This is the truest form of happiness and sanctuary. I wish that I could remain in this state forever. I feel like a warmed place-setting folded into a napkin.

But my mind, it is not working, so I try to count sheep, pull at ingrown hairs, toss and turn. I am consumed by Adrieneese, the memory of Adrieneese, her body, her moist lips, her tender smile, her careful words. Since I am perfectly contained within the bed, with toes curled, I make a list instead. The list stems from one nightmarish thought: Adrieneese getting married!

List of Things I Couldn't Handle: Not now, not ever!

1. Adrieneese gets married to a hot Latino musician.

2. Baby expected.

3. Adrieneese is short of cash and asks me to repay money lent out over period of relationship. But since I'm skint she opts to sue.

4. Momee objects to daughter's out-of-pocket

state by bringing along Maria and all her exboyfriends; they protest outside the door banging on pots and pans. Landlady sticks her head out the window, cries: "Is this about money?" The neighbours object, then sympathize and join in. A steaming, bobbing, heady mass of open mouths, raised fists. Madness ensues when a local dissident group joins in the melee. They start broadcasting live, a man with a megaphone SHOUTS and people who haven't seen each other in years exchange phone numbers. I peer out the window: Write on the back of a mouldy two-four of Keith's beer and pitch it out: GO AWAY! I AM NOT COMING OUT. The mass just amplifies and people stare and stare. This zombification intensifies with the arrival of a bored Maury and a humoured, self-righteous Shand, who tries to scale the walls of the apartment and break in.

5. I don't let them in. I retreat to the toilet.

FIFTY-FOUR

I decide that I am gong to write a letter to Elliott. It is going to be the perfect letter: the perfect statement of everything I believe. He will then know exactly what he needs to know—that he cannot buy me or anyone else. I am not a member of his film club; I am not available to be hired out at kids' parties; I am not a dancing fool, a clown. I am my mother's son, my sister's brother. I am a careful, kind person and yes I am broke but I do, actually, care more for the state of the world than might presently appear.

Dear Elliott:
    But then a deluded guilt factor kicks in…
    Who the hell am I to say this shit?

FIFTY-FIVE

I wonder what his goddamned astrological sign is? Probably a Pisces—I've never been able to trust them. Or a Taurus, overbearing and manipulative. A bull with giant horns behind the wheel of his great monster Rolls-Royce bashing its way down our packed street. Parking tickets and violation slips peel off the windshield and sail like feathers into the wind as he comes along. I slide back into the house and tiptoe up the stairs. The bastard is hammering on the door. Yelling, up the stairs. Hammering away into his cellphone.
    I look down from the balcony ready to drop a plant on his head. Elliott yelling. Screaming. *Give me back the money that I have invested in developing you! Give me back the time I have spent with you!*
    Bugger it. I cannot sell him on optioning my own short story. What are the odds that he'll even read it? I'll have to show him that he's got the wrong man; he needs a TV hack.

So, fuck the sci-fi idea. I must demand that he find a different subject. What, though? Divorce? No, I don't have the experience (not officially, anyhow). Alcoholism? No... (too boring, plus Elliott might sue).

Something obscure, like... poetry. Why not? Poetry interests me. Poets are strange chaps (an easy out), and can win the hearts of women! I need to win the heart of Adrieneese. When Ade sees this film she will see what she has done to me; there will be code there, a secret code for her to obsess and wonder about. Once a woman leaves that's it, they say, but if the poor bastard reinvents himself as... an entity, a famous being, he's not the same bastard is he?

Plus this will really get Elliott: it will be my revenge.

So I'm going to write about a famous New York poet named Richard Caple. I am going to write that he has dropped out of the New York literary scene because of a failed romance and has emerged as a lonely janitor in a Toronto dancehall. Richard Caple is going to be the antithesis of myself: a success! Will Elliott detect the irony?

What if Caple is rediscovered by an emerging writer, based on self? We'll call the struggling writer "Gordo," so that Elliott cannot tell it is actually me. What if the struggling writer convinces the old poet to front a rock and roll band? Ha ha! Elliott! Let's see you film this!

Part Three

The poet is like the prince of the clouds
who rides the tempest and scorns the archer.
Exiled on the ground, amidst boos and insults,
his giant wings prevent his walking.
—Charles Baudelaire

FIFTY-SIX

The screenplay is called *Prince of the Clouds*. It is going to be a nightmare to film, and character-based. Elliott is going to flip.

I attack this screenplay, convinced it is either masterpiece or bowel towel depending on the number of coffees I've inhaled and how many times I've stared at the phrases "cut to," "slug line," so forth and such like. I could very well take up smoking cigarettes instead of finishing this but I also need to get Adrieneese back, and don't think she would approve of my inertia and fixating.

Instead of smoking or abusing myself, I read a literary magazine I like because it is basic and sports a single but different colour each issue, and says *Rude Bits* at the top of it. I go straight for the reviews section and get through four reviews of small press books in which some self-congratulatory hack—after first making reference to a poetry chapbook "in its fifth printing"—praises how "it moved" him with "grace and beauty."

These are the deadwood phrases of book reviews and I hate them because they could describe any crap little poetry book, and do. I remember that I heard a writer say on the radio that writers write because they don't want to change their shoes. I think of saggy-assed and drained-looking mopers in Tilly's.

Then me, hunched over a fading computer screen. Yuck.

FIFTY-SEVEN

Back to this screenplay. This statement of contempt for Elliott and the two thousand dollars he is paying me to write for him.

INT. TAVERN, POETRY READING—NIGHT

A dying tavern-like establishment. Could have been a happening spot in its time—the 1970s but it is now dead. Dead atmosphere. An exceptionally bored and boring man sits at a mic which kicks in and out as he sips his drink and reads in a Meryn Cadell way.

          MIDDLING POET
Disdain of quiet tremors
Sick and feeble whimpers
Of puppies dying in their boxes

A man coughs in the audience.

CUT TO:

A man. The man is RICHARD CAPLE. The former poet laureate of New York. Still in command of his faculties. He has confidence, poise. But he is in a pirate suit. He watches attentively.

CUT TO:

An equally bored HOST takes the microphone.

> HOST
> And now we have Gord. Gordo, everyone.

CUT TO:

Tables of middle-aged female poets. They clap tiredly.

CUT TO:

Our NARRATOR, a feckless loser, stands slowly and solemnly and takes the microphone.

> GORDO
> I would like to dedicate this to the author of *Confederacy of Dunces*.

CUT TO:

The pirate, RICHARD, stands up excitedly.

> RICHARD
> Speak man. Speak.

CUT TO:

>   GORDO
> This from my novel-in-progress:
> "I wanted in my heart to be a decent
> sort but I also knew that my skill as a
> writer had progressed so that I became a
> curmudgeon. A hermit."

There is an even greater pallor of gloom over the place.

>   OLDER WOMAN POET
> This is a poetry reading. Read poetry not
> fiction!

CUT TO:

Richard, nonplussed, brandishes his umbrella like a pirate's sword.

>   RICHARD
> Nonsense, woman. There hasn't been a
> word of poetry spoken here tonight.

CUT TO:

Two female poets whisper.

>   OLDER WOMAN POET
> Who is that man?

                    OTHER OLDER WOMAN POET
          I don't know.

CUT TO:

The host takes the microphone.

                    HOST
          Anyone else for the open stage this
          evening?

CUT TO:

Richard struggles to get up.

                    RICHARD
          I shall read *about* poetry.

CUT TO:

The two women sip from their drinks, simultaneously.

CUT TO:

Richard points his umbrella at the stage.

RICHARD
"The poet is like the Prince of the Clouds
who rides the tempest and scorns the archer.
Exiled on the ground, amidst boos and insults,
his giant wings prevent his walking."

(pause)
Charles Baudelaire.

The two women at the side jeer.

OLDER WOMAN POET
Pretentious!

OTHER OLDER WOMAN POET
Foul! Read your own.

RICHARD
I will not pretend to be a poet.

OTHER OLDER WOMAN POET
Then what are you?

A COLLEGE KID from the bar watches.

COLLEGE KID
A pirate!

Laughter ensues. Richard stands awkwardly.

                    COLLEGE KID
Get off the stage!

The host takes the microphone.

                         HOST
Thank you, Richard.

FIFTY-EIGHT

I am in my room. The phone has not rung for days and perhaps for the first time, I wish it would. I go at the boxes that have accumulated underneath my desk and get stuck there, like an old woman with new spectacles going through an old hope chest. In one sealed-off box I find a note written on a placemat from an old haunt. Written in pencil, it is a love note from Adrieneese. There are more of them, all carefully annotated, compacted and wrapped tight in elastic. They are so passionate and hungry that I can hardly believe I was involved in such a thing. And the notes I wrote in response were probably worse: crazy, sad, and equally hungry.
   I go through the lot, lost in this past life of poems written to self, ideas for names for children Adrieneese and I talked of having. There is a sheet of paper with crayon colouring on the borders, a poem from e.e. Cummings, music magazines from England. There are old résumés drafted while in university. I rummage through with a serious level of ill humour and realize

why I am writing this story for Elliott about Richard Caple.

Yes, Richard Caple is the polar opposite of me; he is a successful poet who has dropped out, not a vengeful never-made-it who teeters on the abyss! He has made the ultimate statement: seen his picture on the cover of the book jacket, then said thank you very much. After tasting from the goblet of fame, he had a moment of clarity and burrowed his head back underground. A failed romance? A childhood secret? No, he simply didn't wish to cater to the masses. He refused to be controlled, bought and sold, by those who regarded him as a commodity. All hail the difficult bastard poet!

However, I cannot let Richard go down. I have to resurrect him and give him some satisfaction in life. So my tender crafter of words must confront his demons. He must fight back, raise himself from his own loss and sorrow. And he will raise himself! As the singer of a struggling rock band!

FIFTY-NINE

INT. RICHARD'S APARTMENT—DAY
A doorway. Richard peers out of it.

RICHARD
How did you find me?

GORDO
I'm a writer. I researched you. I'm also a

fan of your work, Mr. Caple. *Prince of the Clouds* won the National Book Award for Poetry in 1977.

RICHARD
That was a long time ago.

CUT TO:

INT. COFFEE SHOP—NIGHT
Richard and Gordo are there.

RICHARD
I don't think they would buy it. An old has-been like me.

GORDO
Yes they would. It's different.

SIXTY

Oh god, the absurdities that come to me as I lie there in bed, milky eyes blinking at the ceiling. I am fixating on a chat I just had with Maury, whom I should have avoided by suggesting he get back to his busy life of writing reviews for crappy little journals. He proposes to move in to help me pay rent so I tell him I have managed to keep Elliott at bay, what makes him think I will take him in?

He says I will just be quiet and write. I will not pester or bother you, I will not read through your journals. In fact, I will call you *King*.

And I say: king of what? Paper scraps and rejection slips? King of dedication?

It's been a while since Maury caught me at home and so I know I'm going to have to be adept at losing him. I shudder at the thought of him in my house. I can see him sitting there in one of my chairs with a can of beer in his hand, scouring the classifieds for property he can buy with his father's money to resell for profit. I can see him taking over the room beside mine, emailing me ideas he has for books and book titles. I can see Maury's inertia materializing before me: a young man in a pair of boxer shorts and slippers sashaying back and forth between kitchen and toilet.

"Maury, can I call you back?" I look out the window, try to concentrate on how to get out of this. I can see a car passing the house. What if it is Elliott and I have a visitor? Can I really truly say that I'd be happier to see Elliott than talk to Maury at this particular moment? I turn on the radio and make like there is another person in the room.

"Shit."

"What?"

"There's someone here from Random House."

"You're kidding."

"They're here to take my measurements."

"What?"

"They've brought some calipers down and are going to

measure my head front to back. They need to know if I have a large enough cranium to be a writer. It's a secret ceremony in publishing."

Dead air. This is heaven.

"Really?"

I see an electric shaver. I stretch, plug it in. *Bzzzzzzz.* I'm getting giddy here. It is like a sky filled with mosquitoes carrying West Nile virus—hovering over Maury, sacks filled with blood. Sharpening their beaks like knives.

"Maury, can I call you back? They're shaving my head."

I fall back on the bed. I laugh, but not for long.

SIXTY-ONE

Oh Adrieneese, you broke my heart and it isn't pretty. I wonder where you are now that you have left me? Are you still taking calls from Momee? Are you still halfway through far too many things?

If you were here, you would not be impressed. This place is still a dustbowl; the chips and chocolate bar wrappers are piling in the corner like leaves. I can imagine you coming back, standing at attention, looking into my eyes, knowing that I will look back into them because they are moist. You would simply say, Men, *then whisper something about how I like having sex with you too much.*

But these are not the only things I think about you, darling. Oh, if I had been successful (employable?) when we first met... Am I now supposed to be a wise, old, independent man? Not a young man with confused feelings and misdirected energy? I don't feel older, yet I am.

I do miss you my darling, kind little red-faced tomato. Can you believe that our passion has been reduced to this? Where are you now? Will you remember me?

I think of Maury reading these letters and laughing at me.

SIXTY-TWO

INT. DOORWAY, BENNY'S BAR—DAY
Richard saunters across the stage with Gordo and other band members all tuning guitars and doing the rock and roll thing. Two middle-aged JOURNALIST TYPES watch from the bar.

                JADED JOURNALIST #1
Can it be him?

                JADED JOURNALIST #2
No way.

CUT TO:

Richard saunters across the stage. A camera comes up to his face. A flash.

SIXTY-THREE

CUT TO:

INT. NEWSPAPER DARKROOM—DAY
A small photography tray. A picture of a news clipping slowly emerges. It is placed on a line to dry.

CUT TO:

INT. NEWSROOM—DAY
The picture is slapped onto the desk of jaded journalist #1. He is reading through a pile of clippings on the New York literary scene. He picks up the photo.

CUT TO:

INT. NEWSROOM—DAY
A photo and headline, which reads, "Literary Star Vanishes After Awards." The photo is of a younger Richard with a beautiful girlfriend. A hand goes up to the phone.

                JADED JOURNALIST #2
    It's him. Richard Caple is in Toronto!

SIXTY-FOUR

When I get home later in the night, I look at my bed with some excitement because although it is small and untidy and cluttered, this is my bed and I love to sink beneath the sheets and lie there. If it is cold outside, I cover my head and breathe hard into the bed until I am out of breath.

In the night the phone rings and rings and rings but I don't answer it. All I can think of is the poor little mouse that was stuck in one of my boxes with its wide black eyes blinking, and the fact I clobbered it with a mug, now bust. I lie like a slug in my bed and pity the poor little mouse. I think that I should have live-trapped the damned thing and let it run into the park nearby, to show Adrieneese that I do have a kind disposition after all.

Then I also think to myself that nature, by its very nature, is cruel and unforgiving. There would probably be an army of cats and hawks and owls lurking in the trees ready to swoop in and snuff out the life of the poor little sod. I list a bit, in and out of consciousness. I stare at the ceiling and concentrate on sleep until I can't take it anymore. When I finally check the phone in the morning, I do not have any calls from Elliott but have accumulated five high-pitched beeping messages from five different fax machines.

SIXTY-FIVE

CUT TO:

EXT. MARQUEE—NIGHT
A neon sign that reads: Richard Caple and the Reactors. Sold out.

CUT TO:

INT. HALLWAY, MARQUEE—Day
Richard, wearing white pajamas, paces behind a stage curtain.

> GORDO
> Fifteen minutes, Richard. Are you okay?

Richard peeks out of the curtains.

> RICHARD
> Yes. Except that there are about fifteen middling New York poetry critics in that audience.

CUT TO:

EXT. MARQUEE—NIGHT
After the show, Richard stands and fends off the assembled SCRIBES.

> NEW YORK SCRIBE #1
> Any plans for a sequel to *The Prince of Clouds*?

> RICHARD
> I haven't written anything for thirty years. What makes you think I'm going to start again?

> NEW YORK SCRIBE #2
> There are publishers who would make you rich overnight.

> RICHARD
> Oh?

SIXTY-SIX

My Adrieneese. We hung in there, didn't we, like two desperate poets at a book fair. Now that I am alone with the hurt and longing, with desperation so bleak and pressure mounting (pressure to finish the Lana Banana novel, pressure to stay afloat financially), I remember the problems we had. We were hopeless, like psychiatric patients wandering through life; we were needy and kind when we wanted something. But in truth, we were petty, spontaneous, rude and venomous to one another.

Oh Adrieneese. It was as if we both waited our whole lives

to steal away home together, and confide in each other that we were both going to combust.

SIXTY-SEVEN

✷ SELF-ASSESSMENT: A FEW WORDS ON THE STATE OF THINGS ✷

This as a statement on being broke, lost, and good but not good enough.

Think of it as one man, a chronic insomniac who values his life so much that he savours every detail of every day. He considers the details as he lays in bed, wondering if the mouse will come to life—as a vengeful ghost, or worse, a bat. Flipping and flapping around the room, in the dark. Looking for a vulnerable neck and a heart pumping with fear. Yikes.

I stare at the ceiling, thinking:

I fell away from the world and didn't come back for much of the time that I was living in that apartment, in Toronto. Every day for a year, I walked the lonely backstreets of the city looking for a way to kill the time to avoid the people I was living with. It wasn't that the people I lived with were ogres; they were just too wrapped up in their own concerns and interests. As polite as they might have been, I resented their nearness to me and my little secret world that was taking over my life.

Sometimes I can't believe what a twit I was. My mind was a percolating playground of conversation snippets, ideas and comebacks and I was the smartest goddamned fool that lived in it, entertaining my constantly adoring audience of one. Madness never occurred to me: I was a genius and those fools who couldn't see it were lesser people, burdened by the cloudy malaise of a demented society demanding that we bow down to the corporate image of the software company or the advertising agency that you work for.

I missed my family something fierce. When I talked to my parents I was their sweet boy, so they thought I was more together than I was. But I also wanted them to have a little peace of mind; why shouldn't they, given that they raised me the best they could?

But they had not failed. In the midst of misery and self-doubt I was alive, loving my life.

✳ ✳ ✳

SIXTY-EIGHT

In my mind there is no sound at all, only snoring. And it is me, lost in a dream somewhere, the sound drifting out into the night's open air and into the trees...

I am sitting on a toilet at the end of a long hallway. Adrieneese is towering over me in the doorway. My head is in my hands.

"Yarud, do you think Mozart was a nice man?"
"Um, yeah. I'm sure he was."
"Why do you think thees?"
Adrieneese hands me the toilet roll. I look up, mull.
"There's books on it, I think."
"And what about hees wife? Do chou thin she loved him for his talen or because he had a yob and money?"
I look down. I am naked and need to wipe soon. I am not sure what to do: answer, or wipe. This is a most distressing predicament.
"Um. She loved him for his talent?"
The girl's face, a red tomato. It is frozen hard and about to crack. She is positively in a state.
"No Jarod! She loved heem because he was talended *and* he had a job and money. Chou numb-nuts!"
"Oh, of course." My head in my hands again.
That voice, rising in pitch. I am about to lift off the seat with toilet paper stuck to my ass and lighter flicked.
"Chou have to have a yob, Yarud! Ees important!"
Oh my love, is this the reason that you have forsaken me? I am tossing and turning in the bed. Adrieneese is there, an apparition with hair like black silvery electrodes, static, come back to haunt me. I think I'm getting it. I think I'm getting it. I'm sure I'm getting it!
I wake up. Is it too late to change?

SIXTY-NINE

INT. RICHARDS APARTMENT—DAY
Richard sits and mulls in his bed.

          RICHARD
I'm going home. But I'm not going to write another poem.

SEVENTY

With the failure to keep a job, finish a novel or screenplay, the failure to keep a girl, the failure to succeed on any front, I take a door-to-door sales job for an out-of-the-way company that contracts electricity for fixed terms. This is my doing, a search through the want ads in a newspaper. It is a miserable kind of job for any type of soul in any type of circumstance but part of me feels that this is the job I must endure because I am nearly broken and must not quit. I can never relent, even if I am growing old and hard by the day.

    The job is not an easy commute. The sales and administration office is located down the Bloor Line out of town, in a shoddy little building grudgingly signposted above a hairdresser's. Since I have answered this ad, and since I have chosen this path as my exit from Elliott, I have no choice but to go in.

    Most of the people in charge of the operation are not

particularly kind or caring. I get the feeling I had when I was smaller and someone suggested I go in for cadets—standing there unable to follow simple orders, yelled at by the sergeant at arms. I imagine myself blindfolded, facing a line of rifles. The rifles fire, BANG. A white flag falls. Oh.

When I arrive for the sales orientation session I am told by the recently divorced, chain-smoking Greek hulk of a man beside me that this is a short-term job and hardly ideal for the bulk of well-educated-but-desperate Indian, Chinese, Bulgarian and Turkish immigrants who crowd this hole-in-the-wall with us.

The people at the top of this pyramid organization are young, university-educated WASPs from Peterborough who hold weekly mandatory meetings and parade in front of the group with remarkable pace and tension. They emphatically repeat that years of slogging and hammering on the doors has made them who they are.

Superior? No, better than that: rich.

Monday is the worst, as it is "deal day" and the lot of the independent sales agents mill around the fax machine and enquire "How many deals?" Since I have not yet worked—and do not even understand what the product is that I am supposed to sell—I clam up, stare vacantly. This annoys the rest of the mob who persist to enquire about my (non) success rate until someone says suddenly, "They are talking of increasing the bonuses. There is room for a lot of profit. Soon we will branch into the gas markets as well as the long distance and electricity markets!"

I watch the hubbub of it all; the bulk of sales agents are aggressive and short with each other. Are they schooled in charity or welfare scams? Are any of them writers, or worse, decent people who secretly despise this work because they have no choice but to do it?

After a session held at a cheap hotel on the outskirts of town, a group of glum Chinese men sit in silence in a small room with an odour about it like dead air. I wait in curious silence as this rail-thin, chain-smoking mob is chastised for stockpiling deals and cashing in on large bonuses. When the manager sees me I don't say a word to him. I feel like a time bomb ready to go off.

SEVENTY-ONE

I am paired with a small, wiry and kind-looking Indian man named Mr. Singh who has a serious and direct way about him. He has large fierce eyes, a small moustache and shiny grey and-pink dress pants that are far too tight. He has a good command of English and a bright smile, though he is constantly "taking one, two minutes" arguing with our supervisor in the parking lot about money he believes he is owed. As I sit in the sun I am watched by the hordes of shady-looking sales agents, who talk fast but with a level of apprehension about them. I am loathe to join in on the conversation. Unfortunately this resistance just brings more unwanted attention.

Soon I am convinced to cram into a small, nondescript van with Mr. Singh and a whole group of Asians new to Canada. I am soon travelling outside of Toronto—Tweed, Picton,

Unionville or Cambridge—depending on the whim of Mr. Singh who routinely spreads a map across the steering wheel of the van as it hurtles across the city.

The group is diverse but we get along. One of the six is a Bangladeshi Muslim by the name of Mohammed who has a dignified air about him and likes to sit in the back and make restrained jokes about the way Mr. Singh drives—which is badly. Another, a quiet Sikh, who seems either highly uncomfortable or very pleased to have me in the car, stares straight ahead, though occasionally he grabs Mr. Singh by the arm and points in wonder at some monster truck or SUV.

Mr. Singh seems to have some good feeling about me and watches me through the window mirror, smiling. "Jarod," says Mr. Singh. "I am loving the cars in Canada. Every day I am wanting to drive a different car."

"Just worry about this one for now," I offer to the amusement of the rest of the men.

Another salesman in the van is a soft-spoken, well-dressed and older ex-factory manager from Gujarat who remains quiet but looks nervous as he clutches his business attaché case close to his chest. He giggles like a school kid and tells me that when he was an office manager for an agricultural multinational company in Gujarat, he had several peons working for him but he treated his servants like kings. They all came out to the dusty airport when he left to come to Canada.

I notice that this man, like Mr. Singh, does not drink and that his wife also has prepared a meal for him each and every day, which he eats quietly in the car. Another in the van is a pudgy eighteen year-old Chinese student, Chinh Qi, squashed in the middle and dressed in baggy khaki pants and a loose golf shirt. He is far younger than the rest of us, but looks like a scientist in his face, with small eyes and an unusually high voice. He says that he feels nervous sometimes when people ask him why he is knocking on their doors. He asks me if I know that the chances of making it as a writer are very slim. After I inform him that I've been not making it for years, he tells me that his father is in the import/export business, is very influential in Beijing and can help sell my book in China when I get it published.

An eager excitement fills the van as the financial promise of this book sale in China is discussed amongst the men—though I can sense as I sit quietly in the back that Mr. Singh is suspicious of the mental energy of the mighty Chinh, as if he is an Genghis spy sent out to infiltrate the ruling dominant Rajasthan or Gujarati tribes who rule over this vehicle.

The final member of the van is a pockmarked and lean man, also from the Indian subcontinent. He is quiet and broody and has a dissatisfied look in his eye. I note, as he asks me for "One, two cigarette, okay?" that he dyes his hair black and has a stripe of red in it. He knows Mr. Singh from another door-to-door job and is constantly telling Mr. Singh, in a commanding voice, that Mr. Singh is very handsome like a Gujarati prince.

This pockmarked man smokes and tells me his name is Sunil Pushpal Bhophal. But he adds, extending his hand, "You may call me Sunil the Sly."

I tell him my name is Jarod. He doesn't seem interested in me until I tell him he looks like Om Puri, the Indian actor from *City of Joy*. His face lights up with elation: a great smile and flashing of the eyes. "Actually I am hearing this from more than one person," he confides. He then tells me and the captive audience in the van that his mother is from Australia and that he has come to Canada to escape his father, a rich financier in Calcutta, who has been trying to marry him off for years and sits like a Buddha in his dingy office collecting money that he will not give to his son. Sunil takes a growing interest in me and he asks, "Jarod where are you from? Which part of Canada?"

I say the East and he says, "Really? Montreal! I have been to Montreal so many times… Montreal Casino, in the strip club, drinking the beers."

Every time we drive by a set of newly developed townhouses he says, "Mr. Singh, these properties are two-garage-door dwellings. I cannot get combos here. Take me to another town. Right away."

"Why?" says Mr. Singh, eyes in the rearview mirror.

"This area has been badly hammered already. By Ontario Energy, I'm telling you!"

Mr. Singh says, "You will work here. This is the territory we have been assigned. And you will get combos. You cannot get the bonus unless you get the combos."

"This area has been hardly hit by the Chinese. They have come here previously, like soldiers. They are the registering soldiers."

I notice that Chinh inhales, slightly.

"What is a combo?" I ask.

Mr. Singh, who at times has a very quiet simmering tension about him, says with some power from the front seat, "When you are making the combos, you are making a lot of bonus money." Mr. Singh is smiling. "Jarod you must push for the combos!"

Chinh, who is in the front seat, pushes forward. "So I am to understand that a combo is an electricity contract and a long-distance contract. This is correct?"

All in the car seem to surge forward, as if prisoners in jail listening to an announcement that will signal their release. Sunil leans forward, though seems bored by this discussion, and is smoking.

"Drop me off downtown. I am not feeling good about this area at all! Take me to the town centre. I will have some teatime, a little bit beer, and then I will meet with the *landlords*. Once I am chatting pleasantly with them I will sign up all of their properties. All for combos."

I am charmed by Sunil, though there is something in this job that makes me feel despondent and depressed. I feel as if I am living my life on the basis that every day depends on working hard physically, and my mind is being left to stagnate. I am forcing myself into the fields of my country, and seeing the dirt and scum and poverty and racism of these small Ontarian towns whose citizens, mainly pensioners and wily old codgers, trap me in their houses and grill me for hours and then do not sign electricity contracts. Some tell me that this job is beneath me and that I should be doing a real job, not scamming my own people. In my mind I am in agreement but also powerless as I have sunk to this level of having to make money, and at least this privatized company is owned partly by the government that most of these Ontarians voted in.

Once I am locked in the house and an old man threatens to call the police. I tell him that he looks like a man I had seen on a television infomercial and he warms to that, though I very nearly shit my pants. When I get outside I note that the most troubling element of the job is that we are constantly going to the poorer parts of the town. Some of the people are so trusting, and *want* to let us into their houses. They offer us drinks of beer and water, and umbrellas to stand under when it rains. I want to tell them that through this privatization scheme, their government is robbing them blind! Corruption is taking place within me and all around me. I feel that I am about to break into tears at any time in one of these small rural homes. But there is a camaraderie with these outsiders as well, as we are all desperately trying to hold onto some standard of living as well.

SEVENTY-TWO

I sit by the roadside after a long day of not getting much business and talk with Mohammed, who walks slowly and patiently and never makes more than one hundred dollars a day pushing energy contracts.

We wait at the end of day on the curb, tired and sore from walking through some rural Ontario town and we don't say much, just wait for Mr. Singh to drive up and honk once in the nondescript blue van. As we wait, there is a feeling that we are not welcome sitting on the curb with our Hydro jackets on. Mohammed confides in me that Mr. Singh has been quietly pushing for him to drive his own car on these trips so that Mr. Singh can continue to recruit more people to drive out into the small towns like Picton, Belleville and Tweed. Mohammed speaks quietly and says that he can't afford to overburden his family with the extra mileage costs. Then Mohammed stops and points: "Jumping, jumping," he says quietly.

We both watch Sunil the Sly, who has a slouch about him and an over-the-shoulder bag, making a determined dash across Simcoe Street and onto the lawn of an old man who has appeared, visibly puzzled, from his shed. The old man listens to Sunil, then looks over at us sitting on the curb. We hear Sunil call towards us and assure the old man that we are his good friends. The man looks over with some skepticism and after some frenzied remarks he turns to call to his wife and son who are in the back seated at a picnic table. "Hitting, hitting," Mohammed says. He draws on the ground with a stick.

The whole family is now on the front lawn looking over the pile of papers that Sunil is gallantly showing them. Mohammed nudges me. "Signing, signing," he says.

Later in the car, Sunil the Sly yells confidently as he takes off his shoes and relaxes in the back seat, that he will easily make the bonus of one hundred combos this week. Soon he will treat all of us to an Indian meal of Gujarati thali at a very good restaurant in Toronto. Mr. Singh eyes him through the mirror and says that since he comes from Gujarat, his wife is making this meal for him every day and that he would like to try something different if Sunil is so generous.

Sunil the Sly is after me next, and he asks if we can "get a little bit beer together" and if I would be interested in getting an apartment with him. Do I have a sister and so on… until finally I get fed up and ask Sunil why he has been selling in Mohammed's territory.

"Sometimes, you have to be a little bit tricky," says Sunil the Sly.

Later when we are almost home, the quiet Sikh begins

chuckling in the front seat. Chinh asks what is so funny. The quiet Sikh leans forward and whispers to Mr. Singh. Mr. Singh laughs, and then frowns. "Sunil told the old man if he did not sign his contract he would cut off the old man's power."

Later when we are stopped at the side of the road on the way back from Perth, Sunil gets out of the van with Chinh and they go to piss in the bushes. A Bulgarian woman who is travelling (chain-smoking) with us for two weeks turns to me and says gruffly:

"Life is easy for men and dogs."

SEVENTY-THREE

It is mainly Mr. Singh, Sunil, Mohammed and I who travel together in the van. Sunil the Sly is continually unloaded onto a street in the middle of a town and the second he is out I see him survey the scene warily for a moment, like a barn cat that has been dumped out on a roadside. I see him on various back-alley trips to convenience stores for a snack. I spot him occasionally chatting plain-looking girls at Tim Hortons or Coffee Time. There is a sad, defeated look about him at the end of some days, when he will sit beside me and ask if I have a girlfriend. He is forever criticizing the business practices of the electricity company he used to work for, and telling us how he convinced an old lady to fax a cancellation letter to the head office of the rival company so that he could sign her up. Every day he varies in his story, but the conclusion always is that he hates this job and how it makes you money crazy.

After a few weeks Sunil is getting so many deals that he rushes back to the blue van and tells Mr. Singh that he expects nothing less than five thousand dollars. "When are the cheques coming?"

Mr. Singh tells him that actually he is waiting for money from his own boss and the cheques are coming late. Sunil takes "just one cigarette" and tells me that he is working too hard, his body is tired and he is lonely in Canada. He also says that there is something soul-destroying about this job that keeps him from sleeping at night.

Now driving, Mr. Singh sighs and says that this is a good job if you are honest: there is nothing to be ashamed of in this kind of business as long as you are always telling the truth, because these products and services are needed by everyone. The conversation is interrupted when Sunil becomes engaged in a cellphone conversation. His eyes and voice raise as he tells a woman that "You have promised me and I have taken you in confidence to pay me nicely and kindly and now you are not doing!"

Everyone in the van gets very tense. Mr. Singh, his big brown hypnotic eyes in the rearview, is winding all over the road while enormous trucks pass. Mohammed reminds us his wife and family are waiting expectantly for him, and Sunil slams down his cell and says he is feeling like he is now cold and can he urgently borrow my sweater.

I give him my company jacket, which he admires, and he yells to the front: "Mr. Singh, this company where we are working has been around for more than one hundred years and still these townspeople are treating us like dogs!" Then he suddenly says to me, "Jarod, you are such an honest man. Your face is so handsome, why you are not married? If you are getting combos no woman will be able to resist you."

I tell him I am married to my writing.

Mr. Singh, who seems perpetually fascinated by Chinese people, tells of how one young Chinese saleswoman once ran back to the van in tears after being chased across a lawn by an old Chinese woman. Mr. Singh tells me this woman was hired to sell contracts to the Chinese community in Markham, to test-market the area. She told him the Chinese are unkind and ruthless to their own people because religion and philosophy had been cut out of their lives. Mr. Singh tells us that religion breeds compassion.

Sunil grows tired of this, saying excitedly, "Actually, I am liking this discussion so much, Mr. Singh. Your father would be proud. You are the pure Gujarati guy. You are always talking of India, eating only vegetarian meals on fast each and every week!"

Mr. Singh laughs at Sunil, and soon the atmosphere in the van is comfortable again. I am feeling good because I have made a little money and am planning to enjoy a good meal when I get home. Sunil lies in the back smoking silently. He remains quiet until we hit a bump in the road, when he yells out confidently and unexpectedly, "I am thinking just now that I am liking Mr. Singh's round ass! Actually many Indian girls are liking Mr. Singh's ass. And his moustache! But his wife is waiting for him obediently in his apartment, with vegetarian curry. What to do?"

"At least he has a wife!" I say, then immediately regret it.

The men look at me, then laugh.

SEVENTY-FOUR

The phone picked up with care.
A voice, grave and gravelly.
No salutation—no kind How are you?
Nothing.
Just the grating tones of Elliott:
"Jarod, I've been meaning to ask you. Do you get any sort of action with the writing? What I mean to ask you is, *do you get laid?*"

I have tried to edit this conversation with Elliott out of my memory, and still it haunts me as I lay in my bed. A thought occurs to me about women and then a thrown-out segment of the Lana Banana novel that has nothing to do with Lana Banana, perhaps because it is about me.

However, my novel is about *love and feelings*. Or, at least these are the things that I *would like* the Lana Banana novel to be about. I feel these are the only things that all good novels are about. However, I cannot just write *love and feelings* twenty thousand times—though I have been tempted to do so.

Just one other little problem. If I could teleport the following passage to Elliott and tell him it was not a screenplay or a story treatment, would he actually read it?

✳ POSSIBLE ADDITION TO LANA BANANA NOVEL ✳

Heddy showed up in third year. She had dark black hair, hips, full lips and a healthy dose of self-loathing. She told me that the female praying mantis bites the head off the male after they have intercourse. We were at a campfire at Georges Island out in Halifax Harbour eating hot dogs, staring at the camp flames when we met. She was only eighteen. She told me about a couple of guys who were in a travelling juggling act from Louisiana whom she just met and fooled around with during the hot and sticky month of August.

Heddy once told me I was not the guy for her because I wasn't a part of God's Green Earth. In fact, I was an astronaut, according to her ex-boyfriend. Heddy told me that one night when she was lying in bed with me, pulling my shorts off.

"You might be an astronaut, Jarod. But he didn't know how to talk to me like you."

"And how do I talk to you?"

"Like a girl talks, but you're not a girl."

"Do girls talk like they're dying inside?"

"Jarod, anyone who reads the toothpaste tube out loud when he is sitting on the toilet is not dying inside."

✳ ✳ ✳

Scrap it. Who would understand this? Who would care to? This section has nothing to do with Lana Banana. But this is important isn't it? I need to say this somehow. I would love to be able to read this to Elliott's barbecue and cocktail crowd on a Wednesday night. This is all that I ever expected of myself; I don't need to develop as a human being any further than this.

But what about Lana Banana? Will I ever finish it?

SEVENTY-FIVE

Elliott meets me after a few months of the door-to-door. He has called me periodically in the last few weeks, but for the most part has left me alone and didn't say a word to me when I dropped off the screenplay at his house. His dog nosed me in the balls as usual and Sharon barked out a hello from the basement, but there was a cool distilled air of having moved on with things, as if he was punishing me for never having made an effort to call about the development of the screenplay.

Elliott has agreed to meet me in a coffee shop and I notice there is a young, annoying lackey with him, who begs money off him, does errands, and is dispatched to buy smokes when I loom in with a large mug for coffee, extra creamy.

Elliott sits there, slouches, puts his cellphone back into his bag. He sorts through his lists, is solemn and direct, and I am sure he is hiding a mickey of gin in his carry bag.

"The formalities."

"What?"

Elliott gives me a lengthy soul-examining stare as he drops in my hand a silver fountain pen which he tells me he promised to give to me when I delivered the screenplay to him. I don't remember this but I'm no fool, so I take it. After this unexpected gift comes a series of cue cards and idea cards he is giving me to stimulate my brain. And then, out from the shoulder bag comes a half-bag of reefer which he also drops on my lap, a golf ball with a film company logo on it, a very handsome set of nail clippers and a lighter as well, which Elliott flicks. Elliott sighs then recites carefully, slowly, a passage that I will paraphrase here:

A spent man lies badly hammered in a bar. A stranger comes up to him and asks him an important question, but the drunken man does not understand. The stranger insistently repeats the question over again but the man is so drunk that he waves the man off and calls to the bartender who is watching, less than impressed. The drunk leans into the bartender and repeats a specific-but-drunk request and the bartender translates the slur for the stranger as being three vital questions: one, I need to know who you are; two, where do you know me from?; three, what do you want from me?

Elliott then laughs as he declares that the stranger is the man's father.

Then Elliott knits his brow and cautions me. "Jarod," he says, "do not spend time with the wrong people."

I wait for Elliott to zip up the rest of his purse. He seems relieved or self-satisfied—I'm not sure which. All I know is that whatever he is about to confer upon me with confidence and certainty could easily be contradicted in the next hour when the bugger calls me from his car to apologize, or worse, make another offer. I suspect that this could all be some silly experiment and have given up on taking this man entirely seriously.

"Let's get on with the formalities, Jarod. I asked for a feature and you have produced a one-hour character sketch."

"But it's a comedy. Unique in all capacities, Elliott."

"Jarod, this is experimentation. It is not professional screenplay writing. There is not one element of basic structure in this screenplay. Everything—character development, arc, conflict—is all underdeveloped and unresolved. I'm sorry, Jarod. You're fired."

I look at Elliott and feel a sense of relief and warmth, almost as if pee will suddenly materialize in a puddle at the bottom of my pants. I want to say: *Thank you, sir.* But all I see in my head is a small man with a placard outside a closed theatre.

The theatre marquee reads: CLOSED FOREVER. The placard reads:

PRODUCERS ARE GREEDY.

DIRECTORS ARE MEGLOMANIACS

ACTORS ARE NEEDY

WRITERS ARE CRAZY

WHY NOT JOIN THE CIRCUS INSTEAD?

Elliott gets up, bangs his foot on the door as he heads out, and finally leaves.

SEVENTY-SIX

The phone rings and rings and rings. I imagine myself as a pile of ash on the floor with little embers like little red eyes, glowing feverishly.

"Jarod P.?"

"Elliott?"

"How about writing articles about your dismal life? Since you are a failure at screenplays, short stories and novels, why not cash in your chips and try journalism?"

I make a little circle with my pen on the table. I draw an owl with a sharp beak.

"You mean like press releases? Yes, I hear it is very profitable if you can keep the job. That's always the great struggle—keeping the job, Elliott."

"Everybody wants to know what it is like to live on the outside. Attempt to explain yourself. Explain why you have chosen this path in life."

"You mean explain why I don't or can't keep a job?"

"Why you don't want to take a day job. Call your column *No Job for a Lazy Slob*."

"I love it, Elliott. I'm going to send it to my mother. Yes, I'm going to write it, but first I am going to tell it to you—no, yell it at you—because I'm far too lazy to write anything down!"

I listen further, not surprised to hear him say, "Double, no ice." I can hear he is tired by the way he breathes into the phone a little roughly. I imagine he is holding his breath because he is so hammered. He is choking on his own inertia; his face is turning purple and he is waving his hands about himself.

"Well go on, Jarod."

I start to tell my story. I don't know why. Why should I try to tell this story to anyone? Perhaps it has to do with the door-to-door job and my determination to be nice and give back to old people. Maybe it has to do with my unfinished novel. The truth is, I am an enabler. I am simply enabling this misery—his and mine. I am persisting to act as a secondary character in Elliott's descent into misery and self-implosion.

SEVENTY-SEVEN

"Elliott, I am going to tell you this because the year was 1981 and things were falling apart in my family. Unlike you who dined on chateaubriand and were flown to ritzy places like New York by your wealthy uncle, we were brought up to say thank you Mrs. and Mr. so-and-so and to clean up after ourselves, take off the plates and help with the washing up. This was the year my dad went on sabbatical to the UK. We all left the Annapolis Valley with him because he could never seem to stay still for more than a year.

"Because we had no friends and we were the new Canadian kids going to school in Britain, we used to play Tarzan and Jane games with each other to pass the time. It doesn't take a genius to imagine Tarzan looked sickly and wan in his underpants and the jungles were a place where the girl mainly stood around bored and staring over the balcony while Tarzan ridiculed the chimp because he was stubborn and wouldn't do certain things for him."

Coughing. A series of groans and then cursing—softly like a dog that kicks in its sleep.

"Hello Elliott. Elliott?

"Jane would stand on the banister and then pinch the chimp because she was bored and fed up of waiting to be rescued. Dar would be in the kitchen below staring into the oven and fuming because the English flour wasn't as good as Canadian flour and the bread was laying flat again. She would say, *You horrible children had better be behaving.*

"Then the doorbell would ring and a man would be there to fix the central heating and she'd drop what she was doing to stomp to the door with her feet covered in flour, and tell him the various things that were wrong with the house. She would tell him he wouldn't be coming around if her husband was more mechanically inclined. The man would say, *Why's that?* My mom would tell the man that my father was an academic, you know, *useless.* The bloke would be back out to the blue council van and hand my mom the estimate and say, *If I had his brain I wouldn't complain.*

"I'm telling you this Elliott because unlike you, who parks your son on the couch in front of the TV, we kids chased up those stairs and had meetings in the bathroom and played the Tarzan and Jane game. It never got boring because there were always the outsiders who lived in the linen closet and laundry room: evil gamekeepers and headhunters and soldiers who wandered into the Land of Tarzan and Jane."

Okay, I'm definitely not going to stop this because I can hear that you are fast asleep and I can hear music in the bar that you've passed out in!

"On rare occasions, our dad Edward would come home looking doe-eyed and forgetful in a smart suede jacket and check pants. He would hang the jacket carefully in the closet and come up in his white shirt and sopping wet brow. He would swing his arms wide and play the village ogre and the kids would scatter and flee through our rented house like fish chased by an otter.

"We all ate at the table, Elliott—*can you imagine no nanny and no drunk, roguish friends around to humour the kids?*—and the table was immaculately set. Grace was said and we all stared at the steaming parsnips and bowls of chutney and cranberry sauces like it was all a mirage that would soon evaporate before our eyes. And then we all were told to say something nice to one another and to tell a nice story about what we had done that day.

"George would say he had left a small rabbit-sized turd in the toilet and that it had circled the rim of the toilet bowl but had never gone down. Mom would laugh with her hand over her mouth and then suddenly become tense and say, *Edward, Edward, Edward, if Gramps were here at the head of the table there'd be smacked bottoms all round! The children would all have to write letters saying they were sorry for what they said.* Mom would then pull out a letter she had received from a neighbour back in Nova Scotia and tell us how the Carter clan was going to go places because their mother encouraged them instead of spoiling them rotten. She'd also remind us that if Granny were there, she would say our father made fools of us and he would be sorry when his grown kids were asking him for money in twenty years.

"Then it would be *hmmm hmmm hmmm* from my father, pretending to do something important with his plate. My mom would stare daggers at him as he just ignored everything, and she'd wipe a spot of grease dribbling down his chin. She would throw a dishrag at him and then it would be back to the Carter children and the reason that these four children were going to be all right was because their mother packed them off to church, made sure they were involved in 4-H and young leadership classes in the community."

I'm going to tell you this now Elliott because I know that you can relate to family dysfunction and I know that truly in your heart of hearts you hope your house catches fire and you can pocket the profit and do a bunk on the wife.

"Dad would say, *Do you mean that, Dar?* and Mom would say she damn well did and then the theatrics would start. Dad would sulk and say, *That's really hurtful*, and Mom would say, *Bloody damn, you wimpy man.* And instead of my dad being upset, my mother would break a plate at the table and run with my father close behind. The doors would slam and all us kids would be staring at each other across the table during dinnertime. After dinner when George and Rachel were asleep, Dad would sit down on the edge of my bed and tell me that everything was all right: we Palmers had to sound off at one another sometimes, which was the way we told each other that we loved one another.

"On holidays we went down to London with the car doors locked tight and seat belts fastened. There were blankies and a small tin of boiled sweets in the glove compartment and rattling, plastic, made-in-Taiwan games that we held tight at our chests. On the way there, there were 'I Spy' games and twenty questions and traffic jams along the M4 and hot stifling weather and Mom with sudden cramps and cheesed-off kids eating too many barley sweets and a mother turning in her seat saying, *Have you kids got your seat belts on?* There is continued fighting in the back and then Mom saying, *Edward? Edward? Edward! Stop the car!* My dad, who tries to filter out any loud, bracing noise, is forced to slow the car and stare ahead in concentration.

"We finally arrive at a dark little box of a pub that is called the Rotten Hand. George cries at the sight of the severed hand in the sign above. Mom rushes into the pub and when she's out she says she's had enough and is going to call the bus station because she can't stand any of us and is going it alone. George is still looking up at the Rotten Hand and crying.

"When we get to the house Granddad leans on his cane in the doorway and Grandmum is behind and her old mum Lilly, who's as old as the hills and near as bright as my dad. My dad will say watch out for his grandmother because she doesn't miss a thing."

Elliott, Lilly would take one look at you and take all your money and possessions in a game of whist, I can tell you!

"Dear old Lilly is soon away to the back room where she sits in a chair in a room that has all sorts of fruit in a bowl. There are flies in that room and Lilly sits there in her elegant but very old way and squirts some smelly mist at them. Dar takes a whiff and says, *That's poison Grandma,* and she looks and smiles and says, *So it is.*

"My sister takes a shining to Lilly and helps her sort through her old coins and brooches that are in a seashell. Granddad will make a cup of tea for the family and Grandma will play snakes and ladders with us on the couch and the dog will look up in a bored way. We will all watch the news on the telly and then we will read the television schedule and plead with Mom so that we can watch the American western with the bad Indians with red painted faces and the cowboys with the white hats, and Grandma will say, *Be a love, Daphne.* Mom will say no and Granddad will say, *You certainly don't spoil the children do you, Duckie?*

"We'll be in the kitchen watching the old man cut the ends

off sausages and feed strips of bacon to the yowling Siamese cat who lives next door. In the morning George and I will make our way to the little back garden which is not bigger than one of our mom's flowerbeds. Granddad will stand in the doorway with his cane and point and say the Latin name of every plant and shrub that is planted there—*Monarda didyma, Lychnis chalcedonica, Potentilla, Gypsophila* and *Eschscholzia californica*—while George and I hide behind the love seat. We will try to steal blackberries and gooseberries from the neighbours' bush when Granddad isn't looking. Granddad will say that we'd better not get too far in the back as he's put windows on the ground to cover his tomatoes and there'll be hell to pay if we break any of them.

"When we are all sitting at a tiny tea table at teatime, there are oil and vinegar in a glass and salad and cheese and biscuits and dollops of chutney and pearl onions. We are all waiting for the meat, which doesn't come. Mom pinches us and whispers that we are not to complain and the phone rings. It is Russell from next door and would we, George and I, go straight over to his front door and apologize for stealing at least a jar's worth of jam from the blackberry bushes. We go and apologize and cower at the sight of the stern man. We notice that there is a small child our age in the back making faces and George sneezes because the house smells like fish and chips.

"The man's wife has a long face and says she knows we meant no harm but can see from our expressions that we are not the slightest bit remorseful for what we have done. George again begins to cry and the woman says, *That won't get you off young man!* I moan and ask can we please go and the man says, *No!* sharply. Then the child in the back shrieks and we all watch as the man turns and goes after him with a small broom.

"*Did you children apologize for what you did?* asks our grandfather and we say we did. Then George starts talking like mad about the way the man chased after his son and our grandfather says that was not the question he asked. That night we sleep but and are told that we are naughty, naughty children. We are to look more like we are sorry for what we have done than we do and though we are told our granddad is very angry with us we still watch our granddad with his pants hiked up around his shoulders and his suspenders as he goes into the shed at the back of the small bit of land."

Elliott, Elliott, do you still think you know everything there is to know about me? And there's more to this! I mean I really could go on and on and on.

SEVENTY-EIGHT

I am under that table, craning for two American bills taped under the tabletop. Two fives, not ones, appear, crumpled. I get up, ferret through my wallet and dump the contents onto the table. Loonies, quarters, dimes and a raided roll of dimes. Not much—not even enough for a beer.

Rough calculation of printing up the novel: two hundred pages times ten cents equals twenty dollars plus postage.

Don't have it. Or even an envelope.

Ink in printer is also... low. However, I can scrape up

enough to print ten pages, but of what? Lana Banana, of course. Ten pages and an envelope and a stamp and return postage and another envelope. I can just about manage this, can't I?

This is the hardest part isn't it? Getting the motivation to send this out. The whole novel could be cock and bull, not just the excerpt. There are plenty of people out there happy to tell you that you are wasting your time.

And this is what you actually enjoy—being insulated from a nasty world. So why would anyone else want to pay for this: you, entertaining yourself?

Still—something inside tells you that you must. You feel a glimmer of hope as you enter the library for the eightieth time that you can—just for an afternoon, or a morning, or in the company of friends and relations—shine again.

And so you finally do it. It slides into the envelope without any fuss. You stand up. Is it the landlady shouting at you because you will not answer your phone? No. It is not her. A noisy over-caffeinated invalid in a wheelchair launches over a speed bump outside. His head looks like it is nailed to a board. He is jerking from side to side. He looks crazed—is he a writer, too?

Stop this. Just send the bastard out. But… which part to send off?

SEVENTY-NINE

I sent it. The Lana Banana novel. Didn't I? I can't remember. I just put it in an envelope and said in the letter that I am sending this out in memory of poor Adrieneese (who committed suicide after reading it). Not true? No matter. At this point, I will believe anything I say, so who's to say that what I write is not true?

I sent the first chapter, not the whole book: just the part up until Lana kills herself. I mentioned in the outline that afterwards tapes of Lana's singing were found and Jarod takes them to Toronto. There is public interest, because she was so young and she had such a beautiful voice. The Toronto media gets all over this: "Lost Tapes of a Teen Queen." People eat this shit up.

But still... I'm sure I sent it. And I wrote a letter to Adrieneese saying that I was wrong and that I have been reformed. I addressed it to Momee so that I know that it will get there. I've improved and I can hold down a job, not just "play games with others and myself." I have found my mind; it is coming back to earth for a short while and I am in the mood to entertain all comers, even be charming.

Except I cannot remember if I sent this manuscript out or not. This is the most maddening thing because it is my mind that I rely on. I'm going insane. Really, I'm admitting this.

I must have sent it. I have never wanted anything more than to send that letter, and that novel excerpt, and so I did.

Didn't I?

EIGHTY

I am sitting in a corner, using my finger to plug a draft. I have located an unfinished short story, stuck into a crack in the wall. The short story is a little parched and sun-bleached but in a prominent place under the windowsill. A rejection letter accompanies the short story. The rejection letter, unfurled from a ball, has done some time as a placemat and has mopped up some spilled coffee—which caked and cracked on the page— now looks like rat shit.

I remember this one and I liked writing this one. I could say I wrote this one for Elliott! It is called "Little Prick."

✷ LITTLE PRICK
BY JARROD PALMER ✷

Rada Fisher didn't work in film, didn't know Kevin Derkison from Adam, and didn't have any idea that Kevin was a lowly PA running coffees for a production company specializing in commercials and rock videos. Rada was an attractive woman of twenty-seven with long legs and a penchant for playing with the ends of her hair, while she changed mannequins in the windows of a Bloor Street clothing store.

If Kevin's mother were to speak for him, she would say that Kevin had a huge crush on Rada and she would refer in glowing terms to this "new girl" Kevin kept talking about. Kevin's mother would talk of boys and girls in the same slightly pleased-but-telling tone that said, *When you have suffered a great pain and you remember that pain, then you are no longer a girl but a woman.* She would smile at Kevin when he asked her about women and she would water the plants and retire to the balcony, where she would smoke a cigarette.

Kevin held his hand over the receiver and found himself rushing as he spoke.

"Mark," he said. "You'll never guess who I'm on a date with right now. You'll never guess who I asked out!"

"Who?" asked Mark, who sounded tired, and slightly uninterested.

"The window dresser, the one I talk about all the time..."

"Did you get her name, Kevin?"

Kevin realized as he heard Mark yawn on the other end of the phone that there were times when he was unable to figure out whether or not his best friend was poking fun at him or not.

"Her name is Rada Fisher," said Kevin smartly. "She is all of *twenty-one!*"

"Rada Fisher?" Mark said the words slowly enough that Kevin felt suitably alarmed. "Why does that name ring a bell? Rada Fisher."

Kevin found his skin tighten at the corners of his mouth, though still coyly played along. "It does sound familiar, doesn't it?" he said.

"Rada Fisher." Mark said the name again, more slowly,

more carefully. "Hold on! Does this Rada Fisher have raven-black hair, a porcelain complexion and a mole off to the side of her nose a little bit?"

Kevin thought for a moment. A mole he would have noticed right away though he would have termed it a "beauty spot" rather than a mole. But he had detected a strange irregularity in Rada's skin while they had been talking—but considered it bad form to stare.

"I'm sure that's the same Rada Fisher who used to go out with a friend of my brother's at Bishop Serpentine—Charlie Fullerton."

"Bishop Serpentine has an excellent reputation…" replied Kevin in a slightly alarmed voice.

"Yes, but schools with excellent reputations usually house students going through difficult times," stated Mark, yawning again.

"Maybe Rada went to Bishop Serpentine on a scholarship," said Kevin.

"Yes, but scholars at private school are easily corrupted by rich kids going through a difficult time. Do you remember Charlie Fullerton?"

"Go on, Mark," said Kevin and he could hear the bristle on his chin causing static on the phone.

"Charlie Fullerton, when he was eighteen, had a problem with women. His father was an ex-cop who set up surveillance offices in Korea and Thailand during the time Charlie was small. Charlie was brought up by a bunch of nannies and maids, whom as he got older, he realized were not only house servants, but intimately involved with his father. When Charlie came back to Toronto when he was thirteen, none of the other parents wanted him near their children because he was *too familiar with people.*"

"That just sounds sad," said Kevin. "How old is this guy?"

"Mid-thirties," said Mark. "Charlie went out with Rada four or five years ago. The thing about Rada Fisher," Kevin noticed that Mark was now whispering, "is that she *looks really young.*"

"Young?"

Kevin put the receiver into his hand. He started to imagine that little pinprick mole on Rada's face getting larger and spreading across her "young" face. This was the image that consumed his mind: that the small red mole was one single red, grain-sized dot that could mutate, grow and bubble, making his nose look like a goblin's and further shrivelling that twisted little pumpkin handle between his legs.

"I have to go," said Kevin. He let the phone hang there. Looked at it. He was sure, and then he wasn't so sure, that he had heard Mark say, "Just kidding, buddy!"

Kevin stared at the phone. The receiver swung back and forth, back and forth. No way in hell was he going to call Mark back.

On the way back to the table Kevin noticed that his pager went off. He looked at the number on the display. It read 537-4606—Mark's number. He turned the pager off and put it in his upper breast pocket.

When Kevin came back to the table, Rada had her compact in her palm. She was applying mascara meticulously—an act that slightly alarmed Kevin. When he had first met her she didn't look the type to cake her face with mud and paint.

"You don't mind if I put on a little liner, do you Kevin?" she asked while putting the compact back into the case. "I feel naked without a little eyeliner."

"It doesn't bother me," said Kevin, as he watched Rada's eyes widen and the lines in the corner of them crinkle a bit. "Go ahead. Put on all the mascara you want."

Rada smirked at him and Kevin was suddenly obsessed by the feeling that this person was now someone other than he had thought.

"I have this spot," Rada leaned forwards, pointing at her cheek.

Spot?

The word, when Kevin heard it, made Kevin's head feel light, his skin feel warm and his vision blur until all he could see were circles growing wider and spinning. When the spinning slowed, he imagined finding himself in a room that smelled of Javex near stalls with creaking doors and a sink that was dripping, *drip, drip*, into a blue little spot in the basin. The mirrors near the sink were sprayed with graffiti and above them was a little rectangular box, rusted in the corners, that had a red faded placard inscribed with:

> THEY COME IN ALL SIZES. JUST CHOOSE ONE.

Then a dark black sign posted in bright red letters:

> THE AFFLICTED PATIENT WILL EXPERIENCE THE COMPLETE LOSS OF USE AND THE INTEGRITY OF SAID MEMBER, WHICH IN OTHER WORDS MEANS THE WATER HOSE WILL LIKELY TURN BLACK AND IMPLODE.

✳ ✳ ✳

Umm. Umm. Umm…

What next? Shall I go on? Is there more to this fascinating, scintillatingly, mean-spirited little dirge? How shall I pen this complimentary, erudite piece of self-fulfillment?

Is this the end for the little prick?

Will the little prick commit suicide?

Will the little prick kill Rada? Will the miserable little prick commit a bank heist so that he can fly the coop, live in South America, act like he owns the whole goddamned world?

Sorry. I'm going off the rails now. But I have to. If you could read it from my point of view, you could gather who this is directed towards. Elliott… Adrieneese… It's clear…

Isn't it?

EIGHTY-ONE

No, no, no. That is it; I'm done. I stand up. I jump up and down and dust off my pants. This story belongs in the bin. I'm not going to finish it. I decide not to ever look at it again.

I address Adrieneese (even though she is not here and never will be):

Ade: This short story, which I am enjoying writing, has the same chance of being published as a snowball's chance in hell *(Note to self: better metaphor?)*. No I cannot do this anymore—write without considering the audience. I'm an abomination with decent hair and legs, and I have no one to thank but myself. I'm lonely, lost and broke but still I am determined to get my novel published because—you'll never believe it—I think of this as *a challenge*.

Thank you for the lessons you have taught me. Oh, Adrieneese do you have satisfaction in knowing that I am so far down? Do I have to show you a map, a plan (pie chart, graphs, budget?) to prove that I am of some worth?

Ade, I took my time because I wasn't in a rush. What exactly are we rushing for, anyway? To have people tell us what to do and when to do it?

I cannot even think, I am so hot. My head feels like a balloon filled with hay and gas, about to be set alight. It is so hot in Toronto that my head, my mind, my body, my foot feels like it is going to explode. Who ever could have guessed that a country with the same climate as Siberia could turn into a tropical inferno for two months? Everything is sticking to me, my underwear, my socks are drenched. Still, I sit and glisten. I stagger across the room, too shattered to imagine how I could get this woman back. This is the reality of being an overheated *human* in this stifling, overheated oven of a city that we call Toronto.

EIGHTY-TWO

If I haven't actually sent this thing out—as may be the case—at least my interest has been reinvigorated, and now I need to finish it for my sanity. I am no longer obsessed with the hopeless pipe dream of getting Adrieneese back. I have cooled off with a cold shower and a beer, hit the desk again and am on a roll. This is the part about the whole book that touches me most—the part that makes me love Lana (and Adrieneese) so much.

✸ KISSING COUSINS
(IN OR EDITED FROM THE NOVEL) ✸

One morning when I was over to Lana's house she was into her photo albums. We were sitting on her sofa and she was telling me how she missed her grandfather because he had gone senile. She still had a hankering to sit on the porch with him and sing. The song she liked to sing was a song he sang to her when she was a child. It was a song about the Second World War, in which he had lost a brother.

I liked it when Lana Banana showed me pictures of herself when she was a kid because she was so beautiful. She looked so happy in the pictures with her parents standing in a kitchen with drinks in their hands. Lana told me that when her grandfather started to go senile, she sat on the bed with him and he would smile at her all peaceful. She held his hand and sang songs from the war that he'd taught her like "It's a Long Way to Tipperary."

He listened and she felt sad, and wanted to tell him something she had never told her mother. Would he be ready to hear this from his little girl? In his eyes she could see the age and the glint of longing for one final fight with a childhood rival, one final chance to sit with a high school sweetheart under a swing down by the river. She looked at her grandfather lovingly. Would he be ready to hear that when she was fourteen she had let her boyfriend feel her pillows? Could he stand to hear that she had taken them out of her bra and let him suck on them? She wanted to ask her grandfather if that was a sin.

Lana Banana started to make me feel nervous because she told me that she started to do silly things when she went to visit him. She liked to play with his hands and cut his fingernails and give him the attention that she knew he would have loved from her grandmother—but she could tell her Gram was tired of giving him. This was the first I heard of this, so I felt unsure of whether to show remorse or concern. Lana said it was a difficult time in the family because they all tried to give their thanks to the Lord at the family supper but some jackass-in-law always made a comment or wise-assed remark about the Nova Scotia Poverty Report.

Lana Banana told me that she knew from the news report that her grandparents met at a fire-hall dance on the mountain and got involved even though they weren't supposed to since they were first cousins. It wasn't anybody's business really; they loved each other and stayed together through thick and thin, and that was worth more than anything.

✳ ✳ ✳

EIGHTY-THREE

When I get home there is a note pinned to my front porch.

The note is written in Elliott's hen's scratch. The paper is elegant, with watermarks and a crumb or two of cake squished onto it. The note reads:
Call me, immediately, please.
—*Elliott*

EIGHTY-FOUR

Inside the door is an envelope from a publisher. As usual I make to throw it in the garbage. I start heading up as I tear away at the junk mail and bills, a bad habit, like picking my ears. I can hear my landlady about to make a move for the door and confirm once again that I owe her more than five months' utilities, so I boot it up the stairs three at a time, humming something prosperous-sounding.

I am slowly opening the envelope as I call Elliott.

The note reads, *Dear Jarod Pilmer.* I am stuck on the misspelling and Elliott is already yelling at me.

"You, the writer, should not be giving me fits! I, the producer, should be giving the writer fits!"

"Elliott, you know I'm easily sidetracked."

"You moron, Jarod. I have ulcers and I can't sleep at night because of you. I can't for the life of me figure you out at all. I should study people like you so that I can learn how to control and manipulate you."

"You slept fine the other day when I *was* trying to tell you about myself."

"What? That you had a dull, dysfunctionally post-colonial childhood and your parents never understood you? Christ, Jarod, it's time to cut out the whining and create something that people will actually want to read."

"So maybe I should write a book about someone like you…"

"I will fucking sue you, Jarod, if you do."

"You'll be famous, Elliott."

"Jarod, it's not fame that I want. I want to film a great absurdist and satirical farce. If we had momentum and I had one fucking clue about how you tick, you would write the damned thing for me in two days. I'd be on the top of your to-call list."

I wish I had heard this months before; if he could make a machine of me, he would.

"Elliott, I have my own dreams. They are as real to me as the day we met and slowly and methodically I am hammering them down and assembling, editing and revising them. I'm not happy in the slightest with the way things are, so I'm writing about that."

"Just a moment," Elliott takes another call. Then he roars back into our conversation with, "You self-righteous cunt!"

I want to answer back, but I cannot. I only have just enough energy to finish reading this letter and open the rest of the mail.

"I'm just about completely lost, Elliott, but hanging on for all I'm worth. I don't know if I can take the madness anymore.

All around me are rejection letters, memories of women who've given up on me and the obsession of writing some miserable, misdirected, self-indulgent and, yes, moving tale about how great it is to be alive. Can you blame them? And I'm holding in my hands the newest rejection letter for the collection, which states that... Um... Um... By the way, Elliott, did you know that I'm going to be published by Second Street Books? Or, at least what I mean to say, is that I might well have the right to call Second Street Books and tell them that I don't wish to be published by them?"

I stop. I can't believe this. Is this really happening?

Silence.

"Jarod, you tit, listen to me!"

I start to sing. I can't help myself, I am singing, I am singing and I am so happy.

Elliott shifts gears. He says in a debauched but enthusiastic squawk, "I'll be by in fifteen minutes in my brother-in-law's new red Merc. I'll have the champagne on ice and a hamper filled with Italian bread, dates, prunes and lobster bisque. I'll take you to the very finest restaurant in this city, because we need to celebrate."

I want to tell Elliott that he is giving me the feeling I get when I'm in the subway and some bastard farts in there and leaves me holding my bags in my lap. Before I say anything, Elliott continues in his slightly jaded but fiercely competitive voice:

"Jarod, I've been waiting for this day because you'll finally see with some degree of maturity that you cannot do it alone. Isolating yourself from the world is not going to make you happy or fulfilled in the least. You need me, we need each other. The only way that we can get through this is if we stick together."

I want to say, "Elliott, I need a *woman*. And I need to be published."

Instead, I say, "Elliott, I'd like to celebrate myself, alone, by taking a long walk." I look at the phone and say what I've wanted to say forever:

"Can I call you back?"

EIGHTY-FIVE

When I walk the streets I take the back alleys. I walk away from Adrieneese. I walk away from the spectre of Elliott. I walk away from the phone, the stairs, the landlord who is still so mad at me for flooding her precious world and the money I owe her and I walk away from my sweet darling Lana Banana whom I know is like an old cat crying for her youth. I walk away from the memory of my beloved but smothering parents. I walk out the back, briskly through the Portuguese and Italian back alleyways with wooden grape boxes and old men digging in their gardens and vintage cars honking round corners and a big, tired Alsatian poking a nose through a gate. I feel alive as I can hear the women singing in Portuguese in the house next door, I can hear the men run out on the porch and chase the child who is six now and not the monster he was at two. I can hear the rough banter of the next-door neighbour who sits in the courtyard and deals dope to the people who come through his creaky gate. I hear the cries of children who are all rosy faces and curly black hair and I listen for the whistle drone of the plodding streetcar as it passes. I know that I will stay off the main drag for fear that someone will see the wretched sight of a thirty-two-year-old man in ripped pants who walks endlessly away from the complications of his life.

EIGHTY-SIX

In the distance I can see the cathedral-like spires of the city, faintly orange and grey and pink, like spoiled negatives. I can see the CN Tower and the needling point that pierces the sky. I imagine the people rising like a wave from their comfortable seats at a Blue Jays game and I think of standing at the bottom of that CN Tower and all those people milling around at the bottom after the game gets out. I think of the natural compulsion to go up that great tall pointed thing and look out at the world—as if I will have a chance to look out over this perplexing, grey sprawl and feel, perhaps, a sense of fulfillment at having arrived at a place where I can see everything clearly before me. I will think of how organized and efficient it all is with the signs telling you where to go, the pea lights on the manicured lawns; the patient men in CN Tower suits will shepherd you into the little rising orbs that take you to the top.

And in that instant I will decide that it is all a big manipulation and that they are lovely people paid to say these things but if they had any sense in their heads they would say no to the stupid eighteen-dollar-an-hour pay cheque, say no to the subway and the tedious transit connections that brought them there, say no to the chocolate bars they consume at lunch and the overpriced hamburgers, and no to tired sayings like, "It's all good," or "For real—the real deal, Holyfield." They would say no to what they have to say *to get by* in order to just get home and be with their friends, talk the way normal people do, laugh and be idiots, themselves.

And when they tell me in a less-than-convinced and less-than-confident tone that I am about to embark on the ride of my life, I will look right at them but still smile and they will probably say, "He's all messed up," or "What's he on about?" Right then what I will do is continue on my merry way past them and the signs pointing to the ticket booth with the tired clerk in the window, and I will be filled with the happiness I get when I am free from the words of those who think man has made the world a better place by inventing technology and time schedules and focus groups, and sold us a lifestyle statement of *That which makes money equals that which is good.* And so I will continue across the lawn to a small door and I will not take the elevator I will take the goddamn stairs.

AUTHOR'S NOTE

This book has been a long time coming. I started writing it ten years ago in Toronto, just back from a tour of Europe with the band the smalls. It has survived a number of catastrophes and setbacks—me first (panics, clumsiness!), then a cross-Atlantic boat crossing, two computer crashes, a computer virus, and an email virus. It has even eluded the skeptical but wary gaze of a boss in an office building as I wrote and emailed it home to myself.

Some of the content has appeared in anthologies and journals such as *Taking the Brim_Took the Broom*, or almost appeared in various literary magazines such as *Saturday Night Magazine*, when I received a very positive letter from Robert Weaver complimenting me on the story "Talent." Thanks.

The first valley part was the hardest—I rewrote this several times from 1999 right up till the time of publication. Some of the telemarketing stuff, and door-to-door stuff was written around the time I struck up a friendship with Silas White in Toronto and his advice, as well as advice from an acting friend, Mark Venturi, was very helpful. Also the "Prince of the Clouds" section was part of a screenplay I was working on the time, on spec, though I was getting paid small money to develop a small film for the screen as well.

Finally, special thanks to many, many ladies I've met along the way. I hope you like the book.

—John Stiles, London, UK

ACKNOWLEDGEMENTS

Thanks to: Silas White, Nicole Winstanley, A.J. Levin, Jennifer Barclay (editorial comments), Mark Venturi (stairs advice 'n' Leafs games), Paul Vermeersch (friendship, carrel advice, odd smoke), Natasha Daneman, Nick Waller, Lee Wilson, Andrew Copeman, Dean Farrow, *The Delinquent*, *nthposition*, Wicky, Annie Freud, *Saturday Night Magazine* (Robert Weaver), *The Globe and Mail* (+ telesales division) Roger Virk Singh, those Grade 10 and 11 English classes at Ecole Secondaire Sainte Famille, Corb Lund (tense chats in back of van in between sets), Gignesh Soni, Pushpal Ghoshal (we are like the resistering soldiers!), Ontario Hydro, Ian Harvey, Naomi Johnson, Lars Kampe, (Tarek... you're fired!), Buds, Susie, Dad, Trevor Millett, (magin'... a sorry), Stephen Dee, (cameras, lodgings, chess w/smalls), Mike O'Connor (listened when no one was listenin'), Ontario Arts Council (Writers Reserve Grant), DAWC Workshop, Maruschka Stankova, Miriana Diquinzio, Patrick Woodcock (CIUT's *Howl*, Layton and other hijinks), Shaw Street Library, the Poetry Library, Hot Docs, CBC Radio's *Q* , *Imprint*, TVO, Much Music, Marcus Robinson (a poet, too!), David Kines, Festival della Letteratura (Mantova, Italy), Atlantic Film

Festival, John Scott (a whinin' wailer), The British Library (London), Leslie Stiles (Lumber Love! 1928), John E. Stiles (family history), Bruce Moffitt, Amy Logan, Halli Villegas, Kim Herbener, Chris MacNeil, Haliburton Literary Society (Euro chapter), University of Kings College, Tom Keane, folks at USPG, Mike Brooks, Priscilla Latham, Michael Hart, Sandra Kirk, Jackie Underwood, Nuno Coelho (karmic helper in perennial job hunt), CSCI, London School of Economics (librarians), *Taking the Brim_Took the Broom*, Todd Swift and…of course, Veridiana Toledo, my wife!

John Stiles was born in Wolfville, Nova Scotia. He has written one other novel, *The Insolent Boy* (2001), and two collections of poetry: *Scouts Are Cancelled: The Annapolis Valley Poems* (2002) and *Creamsicle Stick Shivs* (2006). John's writing has appeared in numerous journals and magazines such as *Pagitica, The Literary Review of Canada, Storyteller Magazine, Taddle Creek* and the anthology *The IV Lounge Reader*. John's music documentary, *the smalls…er whatever*, appeared on MuchMusic and film festivals across Canada. A documentary film about his life as a writer, *Scouts Are Cancelled* also appeared at Toronto's Hot Docs and other festivals, and won the Atlantic Film Festival's top documentary prize. He currently lives in London, UK.